The Jaguar rocketed forw... screech of tyres as Makepeace did a sharp turn into the entrance of the car park.

The gloomy, cavernous space was empty except for the Daimler and the two motorbikes.

Both the black-clad men turned as they heard the Jaguar . . . Makepeace glimpsed one of them pull something from his pocket. There was a flicker of red flame and suddenly the windscreen went white.

'Jesus!' cried Dempsey. 'A bloody machine-gun!'

The windshield shattered into powdery fragments, giving Makepeace a good view of the concrete pillar dead ahead.

The Jaguar ploughed into it . . .

Also available from Futura

JOHN RAYMOND

DEMPSEY AND MAKEPEACE

Blind Eye

Based on the original screenplays by
Jesse Carr-Martindale and
Neil Rudyard

Futura

A Futura Book

ISBN 0 7088 2734 9

Typeset, printed and bound in Great Britain by
Hazell Watson & Viney Limited,
Member of the BPCC Group,
Aylesbury, Bucks

Futura Publications
A Division of
Macdonald & Co (Publishers) Ltd
Maxwell House
74 Worship Street
London EC2A 2EN
A BPCC plc Company

CHAPTER ONE

Chief Superintendent Gordon Spikings, of S.I.10, didn't notice he was being followed.

His shadow, a bland-faced man in his early thirties wearing a rumpled blue suit, had been following him ever since he'd left his block of flats in Liverpool Road and begun the ten minute walk to the Highbury and Islington tube station.

It was 7.55 a.m. when Spikings, after stopping to buy his usual copies of *The Times*, the *Daily Telegraph* and the *Sun*, stepped onto the escalator leading down to the Victoria Line platform. He slipped the three newspapers into his thin, black briefcase.

Behind him the bland-faced man also began his descent. He was carrying a briefcase that was the exact duplicate of Spikings'.

The platform was crowded. The rush hour was well underway. Young girls in short summer dresses were in profusion. Spikings, a heavy-set, bulldog of a man in his early fifties, couldn't help surreptitiously eyeing the girl standing in front of him. From the back, at least, she was a stunner – her short white skirt revealing the most perfect pair of long tanned legs that Spikings had ever seen.

He gave a silent sigh. He would be glad when this particularly hot summer was over and all these distractions of the flesh were no longer around. He had enough to worry about without being reminded of his age every time he walked along a street or used the tube. Roll on winter.

A few yards up the platform stood the man in the rumpled blue suit. He ignored the young girls surrounding him. His eyes were fixed on Spikings.

5

When the rush of stale air and accompanying rumble announced the approach of a tube train he edged himself closer to the Chief Superintendent . . .

The train roared into the station and braked. The doors hissed open. Spikings shouldered his way on board, using his bulk to ensure that he won the race to one of the few empty seats in the carriage. Though he liked to think of himself as a chivalrous man his sense of chivalry didn't extend to giving women his seat on tube trains, no matter how young and attractive they might be.

Spikings took possession of his seat with the air of a surly dog challenging anyone to steal his bone. The seat opposite him was taken by the girl who'd been standing in front of him on the platform and he was gratified to see that her front view even surpassed the promise of her rear-side. She was really something out of the ordinary. With her long black hair, patrician features and flawless, tanned skin she looked like a Red Indian princess. In fact she was so good-looking that Spikings, his spirits momentarily lifted, almost smiled out of sheer pleasure. But then the rest of the carriage filled up and she was obscured by several lesser mortals.

Spikings turned his attention to his briefcase. He removed *The Times* from it, then set the case down on the floor by his feet.

The bland-faced man was standing almost in front of him. When the train lurched into movement again a girl beside him lost her balance and stepped, hard, on the man's foot. He didn't seem to notice and ignored her muttered apology. For a brief moment she stared straight into his eyes and what she saw in them disturbed her for a reason she couldn't define.

When the train pulled into King's Cross there was the inevitable struggle as the people trying to get off had to negotiate both those getting on and the ones who were simply standing there blocking the way.

One such stationary obstacle, the girl who had stepped on the man's foot, suddenly experienced a violent shove in the small of her back. She squealed and fell right on top of Spikings, one of her hands punching a ragged hole through his *Times*.

He glared at her as he took hold of her arm to assist her up.

'I'm sorry,' she blurted, her face going red, 'Someone pushed me . . .'

Spikings grunted and surveyed the mangled remains of his newspaper. No use trying to read the rest of it in that condition, he decided. He'd read the *Sun* instead.

The girl, meanwhile, had found a vacant seat and he now had a plain view again of the Indian princess sitting opposite.

The doors slid shut and the train moved off.

On the platform the man in the rumpled suit watched the silver tube train disappear into the tunnel; then he slowly began counting under his breath . . .

As Spikings reached down for his briefcase he caught the eye of the exotic creature opposite and decided that perhaps he'd better take out the *Daily Telegraph* instead of the *Sun*. He picked up the case and immediately frowned. Either he was imagining things or the briefcase had become a lot heavier than it was a short time ago. He hefted it a couple of times before laying it warily on his lap.

It wasn't his imagination. The case had gained at least an extra two pounds. But how? He stared at it worriedly, his fingers hovering over the catches. It looked like his briefcase but . . .

All his policeman's instincts were now fully aroused. He had a good idea what had happened and as the implications sunk in, a cold, sick feeling began to spread up his spine.

Automatically he glanced up at the red 'Emergency Stop' handle. He started to get up then sat back down again. Pull yourself together, Gordon lad! he told himself angrily. All of London's tube trains were plastered with police notices warning the public not to do the very thing he'd been about to do. The last thing you want if you really are sharing the carriage with a bomb is to be stuck in a bloody tunnel with no means of escape.

A bomb. The word echoed through his mind like mental thunder. He wanted to fling the case as far away from himself as he could but he forced himself to sit there calmly with the damn thing on his lap.

The train hurtled on down the tunnel. Spikings had never realized before what a vast distance there was between King's Cross and Euston. The short journey was taking forever.

He couldn't help picturing what two pounds of explosive would do within the enclosed space of the tube carriage. He'd seen the aftermath of terrorist explosions before; seen the gruesome havoc that bombs can wreak on fragile flesh and blood.

He glanced at the girl sitting opposite and saw her as a blood-soaked mess, with great chunks missing from those perfect legs and a gaping hole in her chest. Even if she survived the blast she'd suffer the results for the rest of her life. She'd join the legion of the horribly maimed, who are forgotten about by the media as soon as the smoke has cleared and the wreckage been removed.

He looked round the crowded carriage. So many young girls . . . so many vulnerable bodies . . .

His face felt cold and clammy. At any moment the case on his lap was, he knew, going to erupt in a bright flash of blinding light . . . Christ, where in the hell was Euston?

'Are you feeling all right?'

It was the Indian princess. She was leaning forward with a concerned look on her striking face.

8

'What? Oh, yes. I'm fine,' said Spikings, sounding like someone had their hands around his throat.

The train entered Euston station. Spikings almost cried with relief. Now if the timer on the bomb would give him just another sixty seconds . . .

As the train came to a halt and the doors opened he jumped to his feet and jerked down the red handle.

And then he bellowed, in his best parade ground voice, 'Attention everyone! I'm a police officer. I have reason to believe there is an explosive device in this briefcase! Please vacate this carriage as quickly as possible!'

For a few seconds everyone froze. They stared in amazement at Spikings and then at each other, waiting for someone else to make the first reaction.

It was the girl sitting opposite – the Indian princess – who began the exodus. She took a hard look at the expression on Spikings' face, decided he wasn't joking and got out of the carriage with the graceful speed of a gazelle. Others quickly followed her. Another bellowed order from Spikings cleared the rest.

There were cries of, 'There's a bomb!' from the platform outside. A woman started screaming. Panic was obviously starting to spread through the rush hour crowd.

When the carriage was empty Spikings placed the case on the floor and headed for the exit himself. But just as he got there the automatic doors slid shut.

Desperately he tried to lever them back open but only succeeded in creating a gap of a few inches. 'Hey!' he yelled through the opening, 'Get these bloody doors open, you stupid bastards!'

But they stayed shut. He gave up trying to force them and backed away down the carriage, trying to get as far away from the briefcase as possible.

When he reached the far end of the carriage he crouched down behind the metal and glass partition by the door. He knew there couldn't be much time left

9

and was surprised that the thing hadn't already gone off by now.

A thought suddenly struck him. What if he was mistaken? Perhaps he'd jumped to the wrong conclusion. He was going to look pretty silly if that briefcase contained nothing but books or someone's lunch . . .

Ten seconds later a powerful blast ripped through the carriage, tearing it apart. Shattered glass and fragments of hot metal rained down across the platform.

CHAPTER TWO

Dempsey woke up to two surprises. One was that he had a hangover of apocalyptic proportions, the other was that he didn't recognize the girl lying beside him in his bed.

He lay there trying to piece the fragments of his alcohol-razed memory back together again. Who was she? Where had he met her? What was her name?

He ran his eyes appraisingly over her sleeping form. She lay on her back, arms and legs sprawled out, the sheet in a tangle round her feet. She was blonde, in her late twenties or possibly a little older, and had large, generous breasts. Dempsey congratulated himself on his taste. She was exactly his type. If only he could remember who she was.

Like him she was covered in a thin sheen of sweat. It was oppressively hot and humid in Dempsey's small flat and he thought nostalgically of his New York apartment. That had been small too but at least it had air-conditioning. Fuck this lousy country. At times it was like living in the Third World. No air-conditioning in the summer, inefficient central heating in the winter – if you were lucky – and hardly any choice of products in the supermarkets. And as for English hamburgers . . .

But there were compensations, he reminded himself, looking at the blonde. And he liked the beer too. He reached his hand out to stroke the nearest lolling breast . . .

At that moment the phone on the bedside table began to ring, its shrill bell piercing his hangover like an ice-pick driven through the top of his skull.

He snatched up the phone, more to stop it ringing

11

than anything else. 'Yeah,' he growled into the mouth-piece. 'What is it?'

'Dempsey? Makepeace. We have an emergency,' said his partner in her unmistakable cool tones.

'You may have an emergency, toots, but I don't. I'm off duty today.' At least he'd remembered that much. If only he could remember the blonde's name.

'It's Spikings. Somebody blew him up with a bomb. At Euston station.'

The words galvanized Dempsey into full wakeful-ness. He swung his legs round and sat up on the side of the bed. 'Jesus! What happened? How bad was he hurt?'

'I don't know yet,' said Makepeace. 'They've taken him to the Middlesex hospital. I'm going there now. I'll meet you there. You know where it is?'

'I'll find it,' he assured her and hung up. He got out of bed and started dressing hurriedly, his hangover almost forgotten.

'Hello, James.'

He turned. The girl was awake and smiling at him. He grinned back at her as he pulled on his pants. 'Uh, hi . . . er . . .' Her name still wouldn't come.

'You going out?'

' 'Fraid so. Got to go to work.'

She frowned. 'But you said you had the day off.'

'I did, but it's an emergency. Hang around here as long as you want, OK? And help yourself to whatever's in the freezer. I'll try and catch you later . . .'

'In the usual place?'

Dempsey looked at her blankly. The usual place? He was going to have to stop drinking while he still had a few functioning brain cells left. 'Uh, yeah, sure – the usual place.'

He opened a drawer and took out his .44 Magnum, which was wrapped up in its shoulder holster and harness.

The girl's eyes widened with surprise as he slipped into the harness with practised ease. 'What's that?'

'A tool of my trade, kid.'

'But you told me you were in the oil industry.'

'I did?' Dempsey put on his jacket. 'Yeah, well, I am.' He patted the bulge under his armpit. 'This is what I use to do my drilling.'

He gave her a wink and left before she could ask him anything else.

Dempsey and Makepeace pulled up simultaneously outside the entrance to the Middlesex casualty department.

'So what the hell is going on?' he called to her as he got out of his car.

She shook her head. 'I only know what I told you on the phone. There was an explosion on a tube train and the Chief was apparently the target.'

Harriet Makepeace, in a white blouse and light blue skirt, looked as if she'd just stepped out of a refrigerator. Dempsey regarded her with undisguised envy. His shirt was sticking to his back and the sweat was trickling down his face. He was dying to take his jacket off but the Magnum would have been kind of conspicuous.

As Dempsey followed Makepeace into the hospital he wondered if the members of the British upper class were trained how not to sweat when they were kids.

They hurried to the admissions desk. Makepeace flashed her S.I.10 badge at the receptionist and told her who they'd come to see. The woman quickly summoned a nurse who led them down a passageway.

Dempsey steeled himself for the sight of Spikings, or what remained of him, attached to a life support machine. So he got a surprise when the nurse ushered him through a doorway and he saw Spikings sitting up in bed and smoking a cigarette. His arm was in a

13

sling and there was a piece of medical gauze taped across his forehead, but otherwise he looked unhurt.

'Thank God, Chief,' cried Makepeace with relief, as she came to the same conclusion as Dempsey. 'You're all right. I was afraid—'

Spikings scowled at her and waved his cigarette dismissively. 'Calm down, Detective Sergeant. You can give thanks to God later, and in your own time. Right now you've got work to do.'

Dempsey said, 'How big was it?'

'Two pounds, at least. Plastic, in my opinion.'

'You were lucky.'

'You don't know how lucky. I got through the connecting door to the next carriage just in time.'

'Any other casualties?'

'A London Transport cop and a tube guard got cut by flying glass but not seriously.'

'I.R.A.?' asked Makepeace.

'That's what I thought at first but now I've got other ideas. I have a strong hunch the bomb was linked to a phone call I got yesterday from the governor of Wormwood Scrubs. An inmate there wants a meet. Name of Charlie Wilson.'

'Charlie Wilson?' said Makepeace, frowning.

'Charlie Wilson was a driver for Tennant, a couple of years ago. He was driving on a big job. Christie's. Half a million quid in gold coins and antique medallions.'

'I remember,' said Makepeace.

'Well, I sure don't,' said Dempsey. 'I wasn't around at the time. I don't even know who this Tennant guy is.'

'Tennant is bad news,' said Spikings. 'A big, fat slug of a crook. Trouble is he's a smart crook. You couldn't pin him down even with a steel stake through his heart. No matter how much dirt we dig up on him he always comes out of the court room smelling of air freshener.'

'The rumours have it that he's set up an American-

14

style operation over here,' Makepeace explained to Dempsey. 'He's got a lot of important people in his pocket. Politicians, lawyers . . . even policemen.'

'Gee, and I thought you English police were incorruptible.'

Makepeace smiled sweetly at Dempsey. 'It all depends on who's doing the corrupting.'

'I was talking about the Christie's job,' broke in Spikings. 'Mind if I continue?'

'Go right ahead, Chief,' said Dempsey.

Spikings glared at him and said, 'It was a lovely job, right in the middle of the sale-room, half a dozen of them, all with shooters under their coats. Then suddenly, as bold as brass, it was hold-up time.'

'And they got away?' asked Dempsey.

'Oh yeah! Showed us a clean pair of heels and no mistake. I was at West End Central at the time and somehow we got wrong-footed – went charging off in the wrong direction. The gang played it clever. Abandoned their getaway car not far away and disappeared down Bond Street tube. They split up and vanished, all except poor old Charlie, and he got nabbed almost by accident.'

'You knew they were Tennant's boys?'

'Oh yeah. But he had the usual cast-iron alibi. Couldn't dent it with a neutron bomb. And, of course, Charlie refused to shop him, no matter what promises we made. And believe me, we made a few.'

'Why do you think he wants to see you?' asked Makepeace.

'Dunno. Maybe he's spent the last couple of years thinking over our offers. And he's got a wife and kid.'

'So when are you going to talk to the guy?' asked Dempsey.

Spikings scowled. 'I was going to this afternoon but now these sods here tell me I've got to stay for twenty-four hours. For observation . . .' He shook his head.

15

'That means if I don't drop dead from delayed shock they declare me fit and healthy.'

'Can't we go and talk to Wilson?' asked Makepeace.

'No,' said Spikings firmly. 'Said he'd only talk to me and no one else. Made it a condition. I'll see him as soon as they let me out of this quack factory.'

'So what do we do in the meantime?'

'In the meantime you two, somehow or other, are going to bug the phone in Tennant's car. He treats that damn limousine as his office. Does all his business by car phone.'

'You think he's behind the tube bomb?' asked Makepeace.

'I'm sure of it. Too big a coincidence otherwise. I'll bet you anything Tennant knows Charlie boy is willing to spill the beans to me.'

Dempsey glanced around the room. 'First thing we'd better do is arrange some protection for you here. Get a few of the S.I.10 guys staked out in the corridor. If this Tennant creep is willing to blow up a subway train to snuff you, then infiltrating a hospital will be small potatoes. You're a sitting duck as it is.'

Spikings gave him a pained look. 'As much as I hate to admit it you're right. But I still want his car phone seen to.'

'You're the boss,' said Dempsey.

'This is true.' Spikings leaned back on his pillows and took out another cigarette. But before he could light it Makepeace plucked it from his fingers.

'Against hospital regulations – and it's bad for your health,' she said. 'Sorry, boss.'

It was five hours later, just after 1 p.m., and Dempsey and Makepeace were sitting in the cab of a big Ford pick-up truck. The truck was painted in garish tones of bright red and yellow and on its side panel was the sign:

SERVICE FOR THE DISCERNING MOTORIST.

Dempsey, who was dressed in bright red and yellow overalls, was driving. 'I still think this is a mistake,' he muttered. 'This damned rig sticks out like a Ku-Klux Klan meeting in Harlem.'

'It's the Purloined Letter approach,' explained Makepeace. 'The art of concealing something by placing it right under someone's nose.'

He frowned. 'Purloined Letter? What the hell is that?'

'A story by a famous countryman of yours, Edgar Allan Poe. You must have heard of him during one of the few occasions you attended school.'

'Hey, don't start getting all snotty with me again, your worshipfulness. Look where your expensive education got you. You're just a cop like me.'

'I chose to be a cop. It's my vocation. You know what a vocation is, I suppose?'

'Yeah. I had one in Miami once.'

They were driving along the Bayswater Road towards the West End. Ahead of them somewhere two S.I.10 cars were taking turns to follow Tennant's gunmetal grey Mercedes. For the past two hours the S.I.10 vehicles had been following Tennant all around London in a frustrating game of 'catch the fly'. Unfortunately the fly refused to land on anything long enough to be swatted and it was beginning to seem as if Tennant did nothing but drive around for twenty-four hours a day.

The temperature in the truck's cab was climbing into the nineties and Dempsey was awash with sweat inside his overalls. But no matter how hot it got he noticed that Makepeace appeared as cool as ever. It was beginning to give him the creeps.

'You're not an android, are you?'

She turned and stared at him. 'Pardon?'

'You never sweat. It's like a sauna in here and you could be sitting on a pile of ice cubes the way you look. So I figure they've given me an android for a partner. It would explain a lot of other things too.'

17

She waved a dismissive hand. 'Oh, it's all in the mind. I think cool therefore I am.'

Dempsey groaned. Then he cried 'Ahah!' and snapped his fingers.

'What's the matter? Have you remembered something important?' Makepeace asked him.

'Yeah. A name. It's Julie. Now if I could only remember where I met her.'

'Who's Julie?'

'Oh, just a broad I know. Nothing like you. She's a real woman.'

Makepeace raised an eyebrow at him. 'And what's that supposed to mean?'

'She sweats,' said Dempsey and grinned.

The two-way radio suddenly began to crackle and a voice said, 'Come in, mothership. This is Crazy Cat Two.'

Makepeace picked up the mike and pressed the 'send' button. 'Receiving you, Crazy Cat Two. Over.'

'The mouse is parked outside the Bones Club in Curzon Street. The mouse droppings have gone inside the club. Looks like a long visit. Over.'

'We're on our way, Crazy Cat Two. Over and out.' She hung up the mike and smiled at Dempsey.

'At last,' he sighed as he pushed his foot down on the accelerator. 'We've got the bastard where we want him.'

CHAPTER THREE

The interior of the Bones Club was cool and dark. Victor Tennant strode into the main bar as if he owned the place, which he did, though very few people were aware of the fact.

He carried his gross bulk lightly and with a certain gracefulness, which tended to make people feel that being so outrageously fat was perfectly natural. The head that sat upon the bizarre body radiated power, arrogance and ruthlessness in about equal measure. He had the face of a particularly corrupt Roman emperor, one that was used to enjoying absolute power.

In his wake followed a girl in her early twenties who was wearing a dress so short she revealed the crutch of her black lace panties every time she breathed in. She had fluffy hair that had been bleached to the point it was almost white and the expression on her doll-like face was one of constant astonishment; but her eyes suggested a degree of intelligence at odds with her appearance.

Tennant went up to the bar and positioned his bulk precariously on a stool next to the bar's only other customer – a slightly balding man in his late fifties dressed in a pin-striped suit. The man turned and looked at Tennant and then at the girl standing behind him.

'What's that?' he demanded.

'A toy, my dear Jack. Nothing but a wind-up toy,' said Tennant soothingly. He reached into an inside pocket of his jacket – a jacket so big it would have been several sizes too large for Orson Welles. He took out a wad of ten-pound notes and peeled off five of them. He gave them to the girl. 'Go and blow that lot,' he told her, gesturing at the entrance to the club's casino. 'If by any chance you get lucky we'll split the winnings.'

The girl stuffed the notes into her small handbag and tottered away on her high-heeled, glitter-covered boots.

Tennant turned back to the other man with an apologetic shrug. 'She has the brain of an oyster but fortunately that's not the part that interests me.'

A flicker of distaste passed across the older man's face. 'Why did you have me come here? You know it's dangerous for us to be seen together.'

Tennant gave him a reassuring smile. 'Relax. No one's going to see us in here. And believe me, the matter is urgent. Very urgent.'

'What is it?'

Tennant reached over and picked up a handful of peanuts from a bowl on the bar and crammed the lot of them into his mouth. When he was capable of speaking again he said, 'There's been, what they describe in the computer slang, as a glitch.'

'A glitch?'

'Yes. Otherwise known as a right, royal cock-up. That untrustworthy bastard Charlie Wilson is after a reduced sentence. He's threatening to sing from the rooftop of Wormwood Scrubs – about you and me, Jack. And to our old friend Gordon Spikings.'

'Spikings? Well, for Christ's sake do something about it!' said Jack, looking alarmed.

'I already have. Or I tried to. But there was another glitch. I presume you heard about that explosion in the Underground this morning?'

Jack's eyes widened. 'That was *you*?' he cried, then in a much lower voice said, 'Good God, are you crazy? You could have killed dozens of people!'

Tennant crammed another handful of nuts into his mouth, then reached for the large Marguerita that the silent barman had placed, unasked, in front of him. He slurped at the drink and said finally, 'Desperate situa-

20

tions call for desperate measures. But in the event I failed to nail even Spikings. All I did was put him in hospital for twenty-four hours. As soon as he gets out he'll go straight to Charlie, you can bet your Swiss bank account on it.'

Jack picked up a drinks coaster and began to twist it nervously between his fingers. 'Can't we get rid of Charlie himself?' he asked reluctantly.

'How? He's kept in isolation so we can't get to him with another prisoner. And our man there couldn't do the job without giving the game away, could he? I mean, we pay him a lot, sure, but not enough to commit suicide for.'

'So have another go at Spikings.'

'Give over! You know as well as I do he'll be well guarded by now. Probably got cops lurking in his bedpan and all. Be easier hitting Princess Di. A lot easier, in fact.'

'Then what are we going to do?'

Tennant placed his big, pudgy hand over the other man's. There was something proprietorial about the gesture, and also something vaguely obscene. 'That, Jack my old lad, is what we are here to talk about.'

'The Bones Club,' said Makepeace. 'What you Americans call a clip joint, but it's a very exclusive one. Mediocre champagne costs a hundred and fifty pounds a bottle and the female company it provides comes even more expensive. But the casino is where the real money comes from. It's a machine designed to part rich Arabs from their millions and it works so painlessly they don't even feel it.'

'You seem to know a lot about the place,' said Dempsey. 'You moonlight there or what?'

'Very amusing.' She stuck her tongue out at him.

The pick-up truck was parked a short distance behind Tennant's Mercedes in Curzon Street. They could see Tennant's chauffeur sitting in it and reading a newspaper. He gave the impression of being prepared for a long wait.

'Actually the club was the subject of a police investigation last year after a couple of complaints,' continued Makepeace. 'But we had to give it a clean bill of health. The people running it are smart.'

'And who does run it?'

'Two Lebanese brothers. On paper at least. The theory is they're fronting for someone else.'

'Tennant maybe?'

She shrugged. 'Maybe. But as usual with him there's no proof.'

Dempsey slapped the wheel with the palm of his hand.

She looked at him inquiringly. 'A brainstorm?'

'All this rapping about clubs – I remember now, the H2O Club! That's where I met her.'

'Who?'

'The girl I was telling you about.'

'The one who sweats?'

Dempsey scowled. 'Well, we can't sit here all day talking about my love life, no matter how much it excites you. Time to go to work.'

'What's your plan?'

'I'm going to sweeten up his gas.'

'Sounds awfully tacky. Should I avert my eyes?'

'And while I'm doing that you're going to be sweetening up the chauffeur.'

'Exactly how, pray tell?'

'By offering him your body. He's sure to reject it but at least it'll be a diversion.'

'Why do I always get the dirty end of the lollipop?'

'It's your vocation, remember? Now get moving.'

Makepeace jumped down from the cab and, after a glance back over her shoulder at Dempsey, began to walk along the pavement with an exaggerated swaying of her pelvis.

When she reached the Mercedes Dempsey climbed out of the cab as well.

'Hi!' said Makepeace brightly.

The chauffeur glanced up from his newspaper and gave her a suspicious glare through the open window.

'Yeah?' he said. His features were extraordinarily rodent-like and when he opened his mouth it was like staring at a poster warning against the dangers of untreated plaque.

'Got a long wait?' she asked him.

'What's it to you?'

'Thought perhaps you'd like some company, compliments of the house.' She jerked her thumb in the direction of the front of the Bones Club. Out of the corner of her eye she saw Dempsey crouching down behind the Mercedes. He was carrying a bag of sugar.

'Do what?' said Rodent-face, this tiny, suspicious eyes getting even narrower.

Makepeace gave him a slow, lewd wink. 'You know, company.'

'Listen, lady,' he sneered, 'why don't you take your expensive arse back to your beat in Shepherd Market? I don't know what you think you're playing at but I'm not going to be found with me leg over some high-priced slut in the back seat of my guvnor's motor in broad daylight.'

'But the windows are tinted. No one will see,' said Makepeace. Dempsey was now pouring the sugar into the petrol tank.

Rodent-face bared his teeth at Makepeace, causing her to make a mental note to see her dentist in the near future. 'You heard me. Piss off. Or I'll tell Mr Tennant you're giving it away.'

Dempsey gave her the thumb's up sign and disappeared from sight.

Makepeace straightened and said indignantly, 'Be like that then rat-face! You've probably got rabies

23

anyway. If you even touched me I'd have to take antibiotics for the rest of my life.'

She turned on her heel, paused and turned back. 'And I'm no slut! High priced, yes, but I'm no slut.' Then she flounced off down the street and turned into a lane leading into Shepherd Market. There she quickly doubled back and re-entered Curzon Street to the rear of the pick-up truck.

Dempsey was already in the cab when she got in and was convulsed with quiet laughter.

'What's so funny?'

'The windows are tinted. No one will see,' he laughed, mimicking her voice.

She shrugged her shoulders disdainfully.

Dempsey kept on laughing. 'I told you he'd reject your body.'

'Thank God he did. Did you get a good look at him? He resembled a deranged Muppet. And his teeth . . .' She shuddered at the memory.

'What if he'd said, "Sure darling, I've got time for a quickie!" and pulled you inside?'

'I'd have shot him,' said Makepeace calmly.

Half an hour later Tennant emerged from the club followed by the girl in the short dress. They got into the Mercedes and it moved off.

Dempsey started the truck and said, 'Here we go – keep your fingers crossed and keep your head down.'

'Are you sure this is going to work?'

'Nope.'

CHAPTER FOUR

Greenwich Park was crowded on this unusually hot summer's afternoon. Because it was in the middle of the school holidays, children of all ages and sizes outnumbered the adults, but there was a sizable number of young mothers in the park, all keeping a watchful eye on their offspring.

One such was Eileen Wilson, a tall, dark-haired woman in her late twenties. She was still very attractive but her face displayed signs of strain and depression, and it was obvious from the state of her hair and the shapeless summer frock she was wearing that she no longer paid much attention to her appearance.

She stood watching a young boy playing with a very large and very hairy black dog. When the boy came running up to her, with the dog bounding beside him, she gave them both a tired smile. 'How you two have so much energy in all this heat is beyond me. Be careful you don't give poor Max heatstroke. He must be boiling in that heavy coat.'

'Oh, he's okay!' cried the boy, who was her eight-year-old son Charlie. He hugged the dog violently around its thick neck. The dog slobbered appreciatively. 'Are we going to see Daddy tomorrow, Mum?'

She sighed. 'Of course we are – can't not see him, can we?'

'How long will it be before he comes back home?'

'I don't know, Charlie – I don't know. Maybe sooner than we think.' She sighed again. 'Look, you go off and play with Max while I sit down for a bit. Your poor old Mum's feeling her age.'

She sat down on a park bench. Charlie and Max ran off and disappeared over the brow of a grassy hill.

'Damn you, Charlie Wilson,' she muttered under her breath. She felt her eyes grow hot with tears. Two years. It had better be over soon. She couldn't take much more. Two years of Little Charlie being without a father; two years of her being without a man. It had been bloody hard on her and it wasn't fair.

She'd remained faithful to him the whole time too. Except for that one occasion with Charlie's mate Gordon ... But that didn't count. She'd been drunk and lonely and desperate for the touch of a man's body. It had only happened the once and wouldn't happen again.

She wiped her eyes with the back of her hand. He'd promised it would soon be finished. Well, it had better be as far as she was concerned – otherwise she would just take Little Charlie and go. For good.

The grubby red Ford Cortina was crawling along the side of the road that cut through the Blackheath end of the park. There were two men and a woman in the car. The man behind the wheel was about forty with the solid, battered look of a railway track buffer. The other two were younger, in their mid-twenties. The girl would have been pretty if it wasn't for her eyes, which were disturbingly manic. Her slim, rangy body was constantly on the move as if she had so much nervous energy building up in her it was impossible for her to sit still for even a second.

The younger man had dark, Celtic good looks. And unlike his companions he was visibly worried.

'That's him! That's him!' cried the girl excitedly as Charlie and the dog appeared over the hill. She spoke with a strong Irish accent.

The car slowed to a halt. The three of them watched the progress of Charlie and Max. When the boy and the dog were level with the car the younger man and the girl got out.

'Keep your eyes on that dog,' muttered the driver. 'He's a hell of a size.'

'No worries, Colin. I can handle dogs,' said the other man. He too had an Irish accent.

The girl was approaching Charlie, who had stopped and was staring curiously at her and the other two. Max was circling Charlie and also staring at the girl. He started to growl.

'Aren't you Charlie Wilson?' asked the girl.

Charlie frowned. 'How did you know my name?'

'We know your da, Charlie!' said the young Irishman, coming up to the girl.

Charlie's frown was replaced by a wide grin. 'You know my dad?' He began to walk towards them. Max, however, hung back. His growl became more menacing. The hairs on his back began to rise.

The girl looked around. Apart from some kids kicking a football about a short distance away there was no one else nearby.

Charlie came right up to her. 'I'm going to see my daddy tomorrow.'

'Where's your mother, Charlie?' she asked.

Charlie pointed at the hill. 'Over there. Shall I go and get her?'

'In a minute,' said the girl with a smile, her eyes dancing wildly. Out of the corner of her mouth she said, 'Sean, make sure that dog keeps away from me . . .'

'No problem.'

The girl lunged at Charlie and snatched him off the ground but as she began to turn towards the car Max shot forward like a black and hairy bullet.

'Sean!' she cried.

Sean stepped between her and the dog. 'Down boy! *Down!*' he cried authoritatively.

Max went for his throat. Sean was slammed onto his back. He started to scream as he tried to keep the dog's teeth from closing on his jugular.

'Tessa!' he shrieked, writhing on the ground.

The girl stood undecided by the car, Charlie struggling in her arms. He had started to wail very loudly.

Colin leapt out of the car, a tyre lever in his hand. 'Get in, quickly!' he ordered Tessa as he ran over towards Sean and the dog. The crowd of kids had stopped playing with their football and were all looking in their direction now.

By the time Colin got to Sean the young Irishman had managed to wedge his forearm in Max's mouth, thus protecting his throat but at a great deal of cost to the flesh on his arm. There was already a lot of blood around.

'Stupid prick,' Colin told Sean matter-of-factly, as he brought the tyre iron down on the top of the dog's skull with all his strength.

When she heard Charlie's frightened wail Eileen jumped up from the bench and began to run to the top of the hill. What she saw when she got to the top made her stomach churn.

Max lay still in a pool of blood by the side of the road. A red car was moving away from the spot . . . and through the rear window she could see Charlie's terrified face staring out at her.

Eileen screamed and ran down the hill, but the car picked up speed and roared away. By the time she reached Max it had turned into Shooters Hill Road and was lost in the flow of traffic.

Eileen Wilson fell to her knees beside Max and burst into tears.

An hour earlier Tennant's Mercedes had been cruising down Piccadilly towards Knightsbridge. While Tennant was making a cryptic call on his car phone the girl had been sitting beside him with a smug smile on her face. As he hung up he noticed it. His eyes grew suspicious.

'You look like that cat that swallowed the cream,' he told her. 'You must have won.'

'Nah,' she said quickly. 'I didn't play. I had a drink

instead.' She reached into her bag and produced the roll of tens. 'Here's your stake back.'

Tennant curled his thick upper lip. 'You take me for a soft touch or something?' He grabbed her bag out of her hands and opened it. She tried to grab it back but a slap in the mouth from Tennant brought an abrupt end to her efforts.

'Bastard!' she cried, putting her fingers to her lips. Blood began to trickle down her chin.

'You can count on some more of that when we get home,' said Tennant as he peered into her bag. 'You're obviously not properly house-broken yet—'

At that moment the car's engine cut out and the Mercedes rolled to a stop. It was only yards from the junction where Brompton Road and Sloane Street enter Knightsbridge. The road was busy and there were immediately urgent hootings from car horns behind them.

Tennant leaned forward, with difficulty, and slid open the glass panel behind the chauffeur. 'What the fuck's the matter, Dickson?'

'I dunno, sir! She just died on me. And she won't restart!'

'Oh shit.' Tennant threw the bag back into the girl's lap. 'This is all I need.'

'Serves you right,' she said sulkily.

'Shut up!'

'What shall I do, sir?' asked the chauffeur anxiously.

'You'd better bloody do something! We're causing a traffic jam. Last thing I want is to attract the attention of the fucking cops . . .'

A face suddenly appeared at the driver's window.

'Your friendly Mercedes repairman at your service, sir!' It was Dempsey, with a big, beaming grin on his face.

'Who the hell are you?' demanded Tennant.

'It's the fickle finger,' said Dempsey.

'What?'

'Fate, sir – the fickle finger of fate. It placed me on your

29

tail in your hour of need. If you'd care to look behind you, sir, you'll see what I mean.'

Tennant, the girl and the chauffeur all turned. Through the rear window they saw the pick-up truck. Its cab appeared empty, seeing as Makepeace was crouching down out of sight.

'That's my rig,' continued Dempsey. 'And Mercedes is one of the makes that my company specializes in. So if your chauffeur here would care to raise the hood I'll gladly take a look.'

Tennant's face brightened. 'You heard him, Dickson. Open the bonnet!'

As the chauffeur pulled the lever that unlocked the bonnet Dempsey started to wave on the line of cars that had built up behind them, then he looked into the engine.

Tennant glanced worriedly at his watch. He picked up the phone, changed his mind and dropped it back on its cradle.

'I can't understand it,' muttered the chauffeur. 'She's never done this before. And she had a service only last month.'

'There are some days when nothing goes right,' growled Tennant.

'He's awfully cute,' said the girl, referring to Dempsey. Tennant just stared at her. She suddenly developed a keen interest in her fingernails.

Dempsey stood up and closed the bonnet decisively. He came back round the side of the car and said, 'It's a strip-down job.'

'What do you mean?' asked Tennant.

'I reckon you've got a blockage in the carburetter.'

'Can you do it here?'

Dempsey laughed. 'No way, sir. I'll have to tow your car to our workshop. It's not far away. It's in Earl's Court.'

Tennant considered this for a few moments. Then he leaned forward and whispered to Dickson, 'Is the car clean?'

'Yes, sir.'

Reluctantly Tennant said to Dempsey, 'I guess I have no choice. How long will it take?'

'Should be ready by this time tomorrow.'

'Nope. Not good enough. Tell you what, if you can get this car back to me by ten o'clock tonight there's a hundred pounds cash in it for you. On top of the bill, of course.' He took out his wallet and handed the chauffeur £20 to give to Dempsey. 'There's twenty on account. What do you say?'

Dempsey looked doubtful. 'I dunno . . . it would be a hell of a rush. Add on another fifty and I might be interested.'

Tennant's look was murderous, but he said, 'It's a deal.' He handed one of his cards over to Dempsey. 'But only if I get the car by ten, no later. And don't even consider any sharp moves. I have people who enjoy righting wrongs – if you get my meaning.'

'You can trust me, Mr?' Dempsey looked at the card. 'Tennant. She'll be back at ten o'clock as good as new.'

To his chauffeur Tennant said, 'Get a taxi, Dickson, and take down the phone number and address on the side of this character's truck.'

Dempsey waited by the Mercedes until the chauffeur had succeeded in flagging down a black cab. He watched as Tennant heaved his bulk out of the car and waddled to the waiting taxi, followed by the blonde girl, who flashed Dempsey a smile behind Tennant's massive back.

When the taxi had pulled away he sauntered along to the pick-up truck. 'You can arise, my lady,' he told Makepeace. 'The coast is clear.'

'How did it go?' she asked as she got up.

'No problems. Your big, bad Mister Tennant turned out to be a pussycat. I reckon you and Spikings overrate him.'

'The people who underrate him don't live long,' said Makepeace grimly. 'Remember that.'

31

CHAPTER FIVE

Spikings, his right arm still in a sling, paced impatiently up and down the small and dingy police interview room at Wormwood Scrubs. He'd been kept waiting for over fifteen minutes so far but that was par for the course with the Prison Service. He knew from long experience how much its members derived petty enjoyment from flaunting their power at the police whenever they had the opportunity. Traditionally, relations had never been good between the two professions, despite the image presented to the public. The police had always looked down on the Prison Service and the members of the latter were aware of the fact and resented it.

Finally the door opened and two men came into the room. Spikings recognized one of them. Charlie Wilson. He was about thirty-five years old, well-built and he was, despite his prison pallor, a good-looking man with intelligent eyes. His companion was a middle-aged prison officer with the complexion of someone who suffered from high blood pressure. Either that or he drank a lot.

'Chief Inspector Spikings?' said the red-faced man. 'I'm Edwards, Senior Prison Officer. This prisoner is Charles Wilson, the one who requested an interview with you.'

'Yeah, I know,' Spikings said impatiently, waving the officer away. 'You can go now.'

Edwards shook his head. 'Sorry, sir. Regulations. I'm afraid we're not allowed to leave prisoners alone with non-prison staff, sir.'

'But I'm a police officer,' Spikings told him.

'I know that, sir, but regulations are regulations.'

Spikings could see it was a waste of time arguing. He turned to Wilson and indicated he should sit down at the small table. 'Smoke, Charlie?' he asked, tossing his pack of Marlboro down.

Wilson took one. Spikings leaned over and lit it for him. He was puzzled. Wilson was avoiding eye contact with him. 'Well, Charlie?'

Wilson sucked deeply on the cigarette, then looked directly at Spikings for the first time. His eyes were guarded but Spikings could detect a hint of fear in them.

'Well what, sir?' asked Wilson blankly.

'Charlie, I didn't come all the way down here to give you a smoke. You asked for a meeting. What about?'

'I've . . . uh . . . I've changed my mind, sir.'

'You mean someone changed it for you?'

'No, no,' said Wilson quickly. 'Nothing like that. All off my own bat, sir. I just had second thoughts . . . know what I mean?'

'Yeah, I know what you mean,' said Spikings disgustedly. 'You've all of a sudden developed a nasty attack of stage fright, and I want to know who gave it to you.'

'I'm sorry. I have nothing to say.'

'On the contrary, Charlie boy. You've told me a lot already.'

Dempsey and Makepeace were waiting by their car outside the prison. When Spikings emerged they hurried over to him.

'Well, what did Charlie have to tell you?' asked Makepeace.

'That Tennant's got to him somehow. Since yesterday,' said Spikings with a scowl.

'How do you mean?' asked Dempsey.

'He's clammed up tighter than a frigid nun. Which makes me curious to know what kind of scare Tennant

33

has thrown into him. One day he's willing to take the risk of crossing Tennant, the next day he isn't. Why?'

'Tennant's threatened to have him bumped off in prison?' suggested Dempsey.

Spikings fingered his moustache thoughtfully. 'No. Wilson's kept isolated. Be difficult job to do. It has to be something else. Tell you what, I want you two to go visit his wife right now. She may know something about his change of heart.'

'You think Tennant might be putting pressure on Charlie through her?' asked Makepeace.

'It's a possibility. Is Tennant's limousine wired for broadcasting now?'

'Yep,' said Dempsey. 'I delivered it all bugged and sugar free to his place in Chelsea last night, dead on schedule. The boys at control are taping his every call. They'll alert us the moment they hear anything that might be of interest to us.'

'Good,' grunted Spikings. He signalled to his driver to bring his car up. 'Well, what are you waiting for?' he asked them. 'Get moving!'

'It's good to see you've made a full recovery, sir,' Makepeace told him sweetly. 'As nice and polite as ever.'

The interior of the narrow, two-storey house in the north-west London suburb of Harlesden was like that of a squat. The floors were strewn with rubbish and the place stank of urine and mildew.

Charles Wilson Jr was sitting on a small box in the downstairs front room. The shades were all drawn and the only illumination was provided by a single lamp with a low wattage bulb. The air in the room was uncomfortably hot and stale.

The young Irishman, Sean, was lying on a sagging sofa. He was bare-chested and covered with sweat. His right arm was heavily bandaged from his fingers to his

34

bicep. There were several patches of blood on the crude wrappings and he looked very pale.

Tessa came into the room carrying two plates of bacon and eggs. Colin followed her, carrying another two plates of the same.

The girl put one of the plates down on the coffee table near Charlie. 'Here – and you'd better eat all of it. There'll be nothing more until this evening.'

Charlie gave the greasy, unappetising mess a sullen stare. 'Don't want it. I don't feel well.'

'You heard me, you little English brat!' said the girl, her voice rising. 'Eat it or I'll shove your face in it!'

Frightened, Charlie picked up his fork and made a tentative stab at a piece of scorched bacon. He looked as if he was about to cry.

'If he don't want it, let him be. All the more for us,' said Colin, who had sat on the sofa beside Sean and was in the process of shoving the entire contents of the plate into his mouth as quickly as possible.

The girl turned on him, eyes flashing. 'Shut the fuck up! I'm in charge here, not you! Right?'

Colin, his mouth now full, shrugged.

Sean handed him his untouched plate. 'You can have mine if you like. I'm not feeling too hot either.'

'Jesus, you're as bad as the brat,' sneered Tessa. 'A real wimp, that's what you are.'

He held up his bandaged arm. 'I've been hurt, Tessa. And hurt bad. My arm looks like it's gone through a bloody mincing machine. And it's still bleeding. I should see a doctor.'

'Uh-uh,' said Tessa, shaking her head. 'We can't take the chance. If that bitch has gone to the law they'll have put an alert out for anyone after treatment for a dog bite like yours.'

'She won't have gone to the law,' said Sean. 'We'd have heard about it on the radio if she had.'

'Nope,' said Colin, starting on Sean's plate. 'The Old Bill usually have a news black-out on kidnap jobs.'

35

'Well, I don't care. My arm hurts like buggery and it's starting to swell. It's probably infected already. I could get tetanus . . . or rabies even.'

'Don't be stupid. There isn't any rabies in this bloody country,' she told him disgustedly. 'Is there, Colin?'

Colin shrugged.

'Rabies, tetanus, gangrene or whatever – I'm not going to sit around here waiting for my arm to drop off. If it gets any worse I'm gonna go see a doctor.'

Anger flared up in Tessa's eyes, but with an effort she controlled it and said in a placating voice, 'Tell you what, you wait another twenty-four hours and if it's no better we'll ask Mr Tennant to lay on a doctor. He must know one or two that are safe.'

Sean grimaced. 'Yeah, and I can just see the sort of doctor he'd have in his pocket. One who spends his whole time looking up whores' whatsits. I want a doctor who knows a bit more than how to treat VD and crabs.'

'You'll get whatever's given to you,' snapped Tessa, the steel back in her voice. 'In the meantime you'll sit still and keep your whining mouth shut or I'll let slip to Mr Tennant that you don't want to follow orders—'

Tessa jumped as a plate shattered on the wall. Charlie had thrown it. As the three adults turned to see the bits of china, together with the bacon and eggs, hit the floor Charlie leapt up and ran for the door.

Tessa was the first to react. With a shriek of rage she sprung up after him and caught him just as he reached the door.

'You little bastard!' she screamed and flung him to the floor. Then she began to hit him with her fists. Crying from pain and fright Charlie rolled up into a ball to protect himself as she rained blows down on him. At the same time she continued to scream at him hysterically.

Colin got to his feet and quickly went over to them. He grabbed Tessa's wrists, but even with his solid bulk and superior strength he had trouble restraining her.

'Hey, calm down, will yer?' he cried as she struggled like a maniac in his arms. 'You want to have the neighbours wondering that the hell's going on in here? They call the law and we'd really be up shit creek without the necessary, eh? And Tennant sure wouldn't like that, would he?'

The mention of Tennant's name had the desired effect and she abruptly calmed down.

Huddled on the floor Charlie continued to cry uncontrollably.

Eileen Wilson sat slumped dejectedly at the kitchen table. Her face showed the damage of a sleepless night and a great deal of weeping. Her eyes were red and swollen and her cheeks puffy.

Her mother, a tall, thin woman of about sixty, handed her a cup of tea. 'Here you are, dear.'

'Thanks, Mum.' She stirred the tea disconsolately. 'Oh God,' she moaned. 'What am I going to do?'

'I've already told you enough times what you should do,' said the older woman grimly.

'But I can't. Not yet, anyway.'

'Eileen, your son – my grandson – has been kidnapped. You've got to go to the police.'

'But that man on the phone last night . . . he told me that if I did I'd never see . . .' Her voice caught and a tear rolled down her cheek.'

'And he also told you not to visit Charlie today at the Scrubs,' said her mother. 'Don't you see, they're using Little Charlie as some kind of threat against him? But if you went to the police you'd bugger up their game, love. Don't you see?'

'Mum, I can't! Not yet! You didn't hear that voice on the phone last night. It was horrible! I believed him when he said he'd . . .' She shook her head. 'I can't take the chance with Little Charlie's life. So no police.'

Both women gave a start. It was the front door bell.

CHAPTER SIX

'How are we going to handle this?' Dempsey asked Makepeace as they waited at Eileen Wilson's front door. Though it was only 10.30 a.m. the temperature was in the eighties and Dempsey's shirt was sticking to him again. Makepeace, however, looked as cool as ever.

Makepeace glanced thoughtfully around at the small, neat garden, its flowers beginning to wilt in the heat. 'Let's use the good and bad cop routine,' she said. 'I'll be sweet, charming and understanding and you behave as you normally do.'

The door opened. Eileen Wilson peered nervously at them. 'Yes?' she said. 'What do you want?'

'Mrs Wilson?' asked Makepeace.

Eileen nodded.

'We're police officers, Mrs Wilson,' continued Makepeace, displaying her badge. 'My name is Makepeace, he's Dempsey. We wondered if we could chat to you about your husband.'

'My husband's in prison.'

'Yes, we know. May we come in?' asked Makepeace.

'You need a warrant for that, don't you?' said Eileen coldly.

'I was hoping you'd ask us in, Mrs Wilson,' said Makepeace, smiling at her. 'We'd like to treat this as a social call.'

Eileen stared at her for a while and then sighed and said reluctantly, 'Oh all right, come in.' She held the door open for them.

Dempsey and Makepeace followed her into the living room. 'Please sit down,' she told them, hurriedly removing a toy car from one of the chairs.

'When did you last visit your husband, Mrs Wilson?' asked Makepeace as she sat down.

'Last week.' Eileen remained standing, nervously fingering the red plastic car.

'You've had no contact with him since?'

'No. Of course not. How could I?'

'You haven't sent him any messages?' asked Dempsey, speaking for the first time.

She gave him a curious glance and shook her head. 'No. Why do you ask?'

'You normally visit him every Tuesday, don't you?' asked Makepeace, ignoring her question.

'Yes.'

'So you're going today?'

'Uh, no,' she said hesitantly.

'Why is that, Mrs Wilson?' asked Dempsey.

Eileen began to look flustered. 'What?'

'I said — why is that? Why every Tuesday except today?' asked Dempsey coldly.

Suddenly there came the sound of a frantic scratching at the door leading into the kitchen. The door began to tremble. Dempsey turned.

'What the hell is that?' he asked.

'It's Max, our dog. He's a bit — bit highly strung.'

'Sounds like he's gonna bust his way clean through your door, lady. What the hell have you got in there, a Great Dane?'

'He's a Briard,' said Eileen, staring worriedly at the kitchen door.

'Hey, no kidding!' Dempsey's face broke into a wide grin. 'That's great!'

'What on earth is a Briard?' asked Makepeace.

'A French sheep and cattle dog. An uncle of mine used to breed 'em in Montana. I haven't seen one for years.' He got up and headed for the door. 'Mind if I take a look?' he asked Eileen.

Before she could say no Dempsey had opened the door. Max shot into the living room, almost knocking

Dempsey down, and ran to the front door where he began scratching frantically again.

Eileen's mother came in from the kitchen and stared suspiciously at both Dempsey and Makepeace. 'You the police?' she asked.

'Yes, Mrs Harvey,' answered Makepeace.

'How do you know my name?' she demanded.

'Homework,' smiled Makepeace.

Dempsey, meanwhile, was examining Max. He frowned as he saw the ugly, still-open gash on the dog's head. 'How'd he get that crack on the head?'

'You're a Yank!' Eileen's mother told him accusingly.

'You've spotted his Achilles heel, Mrs Harvey,' said Makepeace with a smile. 'But try to overlook it.'

'How can a Yank be a copper? I mean here in this country?' asked Mrs Harvey, staring hard at Dempsey.

'With great difficulty,' answered Makepeace.

'I still want to know how he got this crack on his head,' Dempsey said irritably.

'He got knocked down by a car,' said Eileen. 'Yesterday. He's been a bit funny ever since.'

'Has he seen a vet?' asked Dempsey. 'It doesn't look good to me.'

Eileen shook her head. 'No, but I think he'll be all right.' She didn't sound too sure.

Makepeace said, 'Did the car stop?'

'What?'

'The car that hit the dog. Did it stop?'

'Uh, no, it just kept going.'

There was an uneasy silence in the room until Eileen said, with forced brightness, to her mother, 'What about a cuppa for our guests!'

'No, really,' said Makepeace, 'there's no need . . .'

But Eileen, taking Max with her, was already ushering her mother into the kitchen. 'Won't take a sec. Mum's just made a fresh pot. Haven't you, Mum?'

Mrs Harvey opened her mouth to say something but was stopped by a warning look from her daughter.

When the two women had gone Dempsey and Makepeace exchanged a meaningful glance. Then Makepeace got up and went over to the mantelpiece above the fireplace. What had attracted her attention was a photograph of Eileen's husband, Charlie. He was kneeling next to a small boy holding a football. Max the dog was beside them. Makepeace showed the photo to Dempsey, then took it into the kitchen.

Eileen and her mother were whispering urgently to each other by the sink, obviously arguing about something. They stopped as Makepeace entered. She held out the photo. 'Is this your son, Mrs Wilson?'

Eileen had gone pale. She swallowed and said, 'Yes, that's Little Charlie. When he was six. That was taken two years ago, before his dad . . .' She didn't continue.

'Where is he? Out playing somewhere?'

'Uh, no. He's at school.'

'Yes, of course. He would be,' said Makepeace. She glanced at Mrs Harvey. The older woman again opened her mouth to say something and was again silenced by a look from her daughter.

Makepeace took the picture back into the living room. Dempsey looked inquiringly at her. She nodded.

When Dempsey and Makepeace left the house ten minutes later they didn't notice the bland-faced man watching them from a Volkswagen van parked at the end of the street. As they got into their car he picked up a microphone and began talking.

'The kid's been snatched, right?' asked Dempsey as they drove past the Volkswagen.

'It seems the most likely scenario,' agreed Makepeace. 'She's definitely lying about him being at school. All the schools are on holiday.'

'And the shape that dog was in — I figure it must

41

have been around when the kid was taken. Looks like someone brained it with a monkey wrench or something.'

'And that's why Wilson refused to talk to the Chief this morning. He knows his son has been taken.'

'By Tennant?'

'Who else?'

'Now what?'

'We'd better go and talk this over with the Chief. The situation is going to call for a great deal of finesse. No thud and blunder stuff until we can make sure the boy is safe. in other words, Dempsey my dear, you stay on your leash.'

'Hey, you make me sound like the Incredible Hulk,' he protested.

'You're nothing at all like him. Apart from being a distinct shade of green he's much more intelligent than you.'

Dempsey grunted.

They drove straight to the 'shop', a nondescript building on the edge of a light industrial estate halfway between New Cross and the Elephant and Castle.

In his office Spikings listened silently as they told him of the visit to the Wilson house. His expression was grim when they'd finished.

'I was afraid of something like that,' he said finally. 'The big question is, how did Wilson get to find out about his son so quickly?'

'Tennant obviously has an efficient communications system,' said Makepeace. 'Even in Wormwood Scrubs.'

'Yeah,' Spikings rubbed the side of his head with his left hand. He still looked pale. 'And I'd sure like to know the names of his postmen.'

Makepeace gave him a concerned look. 'Are you feeling all right, sir?'

42

'It's nothing. Just a headache. And my ears are still ringing from that God-awful bang in the tube.'

'So what's the plan of action?' asked Dempsey. 'How are we going to handle this? Put pressure on the wife to make her tell us all she knows? She must have seen something when the kid was snatched. And I don't think it would take much to make her fold.'

'I'd prefer to go straight to the source of the infection,' said Spikings coldly. 'I want him picked up and brought here to the shop. Then we work him over good and proper.'

'Tennant?' Makepeace frowned. 'Sounds rather drastic to me, sir. And what if he just refuses to talk? We can't charge him with anything yet so we'd have to let him go.'

'We keep him here until he does talk,' said Spikings. 'And just the fact of taking him out of circulation will be to our advantage. His disappearance will worry the shit out of his people and the strains should become visible pretty quickly.'

Dempsey nodded eagerly. 'Hey, I like it. Shall we go grab the creep right now?'

'I wish you could, but I'm going to need special dispensation from the Commander to swing an operation like this.' Spikings got up and reached for his jacket. 'I'll go see him. You two go see if control have Tennant's current location pinned down. Be ready to move as soon as I give the word.'

While Spikings took the lift to the top floor where the office of S.I.10's Commander was located, Dempsey and Makepeace went to the control room.

After greeting the four operators who sat in S.I.10's electronic nerve-centre, which was continually receiving and processing information being sent from all over London as well as from police forces in other parts of the country, Dempsey asked if anything had been picked up from Tennant's Mercedes.

'Not yet,' said the operator in charge of monitoring

43

the bug. 'Tennant's making a late start today. According to the surveillance squad he hasn't budged from the house yet.'

'Shit,' muttered Dempsey. 'I wish we had a bug in there as well.' He turned to Makepeace. 'Come on, let's go grab a coffee while we're waiting.'

As they walked along the corridor towards their office Makepeace said, 'I can't help thinking about that poor little Wilson boy in the hands of someone like Tennant.'

'I know what you mean. I can't wait to pull in that pox bag. I guarantee he'll tell us where he's keeping the kid in less than an hour.'

'Don't bet on it. He's a cool customer. And dangerous. Anyone who'd plant a bomb in an Underground train is capable of anything.'

The Commander of S.I.10 gave Spikings a beaming grin and motioned him to the comfortable looking leather chair in front of a broad desk. He was a slightly balding man in his late fifties. He wore a pin-striped suit.

'Good morning, Jack,' said Spikings as he sat down.

CHAPTER SEVEN

Charlie Wilson blinked in the bright sunlight. He looked at the unmarked Transit van sitting in the prison courtyard, then at Edwards. The prison officer appeared uneasy and Wilson didn't like that.

'What's this all about? Where am I going?' he asked.

'Search me, Wilson. I just follow orders.'

He opened the rear doors of the van and motioned Wilson to get in. Wilson just stood there.

'I want to speak to the Governor.'

'Out of the question. Get in.'

Reluctantly, Wilson climbed into the van.

Edwards slammed the doors shut and locked them. Then he hit the side of the vehicle with his fist. It began to move off.

The Commander's smile was almost patronizing. 'Gordon, please see my side of it. I can't issue a Code 66 on Tennant just like that. Those things are political dynamite and must be used sparingly. The Press ever gets to hear about them and there wouldn't be enough left of my guts to make a good pair of garters.'

'You've issued sixty-sixes before.'

'But on a hell of a lot more evidence than you've got for me on this one. You've got nothing solid on him yet, just a load of suspicions.'

'Suspicions!' Spikings fought to keep control of him temper. 'You call it a suspicion he tried to blow me up on a tube train?'

'But you don't know that Tennant was behind that,' said the Commander patiently. 'It could be the I.R.A., as the newspapers are saying. You've been involved in enough anti-terrorist operations to have made enemies among that bunch of bastards.'

Spikings rubbed the side of his head wearily. 'But don't you see, sir, it all fits together. Charlie Wilson asks to talk to me and right away I'm almost splattered all over the Victoria line. Now the only possible thing Wilson could want to talk to me about is Tennant. And when the bomb doesn't get me, Tennant grabs Wilson's boy to shut him up . . .'

The Commander frowned and held up a hand. 'Whoa, Gordon, what's this about a kidnapping?'

Spikings told him about Dempsey and Makepeace's visit to Eileen Wilson. When he'd finished the Commander said, 'Just more suspicions, Gordon. You said yourself your two officers just think the Wilson boy has been kidnapped; they don't know for sure yet.'

'Yes, but . . .'

Spikings was interrupted by one of the three phones on the Commander's desk starting to ring. It was the blue one, his direct private line.

'Excuse me, Gordon,' he said and picked it up. Spikings waited impatiently as the Commander took the call. He didn't pay much attention – he was too concerned with trying to think up a really persuasive argument to convince him to issue the Code 66 – but he did notice that it seemed a very one-sided conversation, the Commander not contributing much to it at all. In fact he sounded almost deferential and Spikings decided that it was one of the big brass at the Yard on the other end of the line.

Finally the Commander hung up. 'Sorry about that,' he said, then he stared at Spikings with concern in his eyes. 'Gordon, do you feel all right? You're looking rather pale around the gills.'

'I'm OK. Just feeling the after-effects of that explosion. Knocked the stuffing out of me. I'm not as young as I used to be, I guess.'

The Commander immediately got up and went to a

46

cabinet behind his desk. He returned carrying a large glass of brandy which he handed to Spikings. 'Here, drink this. You look as if you could do with it.'

Even though he didn't want it Spikings decided to accept the brandy to keep the Commander happy. As he sipped it the Commander sat down again and leaned back in his chair. 'All right Gordon, why don't you run through the whole thing again and we'll see if we can sort it out.'

With a sigh Spikings began to explain for the second time why he believed Tennant was his number one target.

As he talked the Commander glanced at his watch.

'Do you ever go anywhere without that thing?' asked Makepeace. She was referring to Dempsey's .44 Magnum which he was in the process of cleaning. 'I imagine you even wear it in the bath.'

Dempsey narrowed his eyes at her and said, 'Do you often imagine me in the bath?'

Two small spots of red appeared on her cheeks. Haughtily she said, 'I assure you, Dempsey, that you rarely impinge on my thoughts at all, in the bath or otherwise.'

He grinned at her. 'Hey, come on, you can admit it. You secretly have the hots for me. It's just that your English reserve prevents you from coming clean about it.'

The colour on her cheeks went a deeper red. 'What absolute rubbish! I wouldn't—'

Before she could continue, one of the operators from control, a young red-haired woman who was a former WREN, hurried into the office carrying a small tape recorder.

'We just picked this up from Tennant's car,' she told them, placing the machine on Dempsey's desk and switching it on.

The sound of a car's motor, accompanied by various traffic sounds and the rustling of clothing and upholstery, could be heard from the recorder. Then came the beep-beep sound of a phone number being punched out, followed by a man's voice. It was Tennant's.

'It's me . . . listen, are you alone?'

Pause.

'Okay. I get the message. You can't talk. Then just keep quiet and listen. First, Wilson's wife had a visit. My look-out is sure they were cops. A big sod with dark hair, and a pretty blonde. Would they be S.I.10?'

Pause.

'I thought so. That means Spikings is getting too close for comfort. I'm tired of pussy-footing around. I've taken steps to pull Wilson out of the game entirely. Even though we've got his kid Spikings might still persuade him to talk. I'm going to take Spikings out as well.'

Pause. A car horn hooted in the background.

Tennant continued. 'No, my mind's made up. He goes. Today. The bastard's been giving me more irritation than my piles for too long. And it would make things a lot easier for you too if he was no longer around, right? So what I need is some help from you in setting him up . . .'

Another pause.

Then, 'OK, ring me back as soon as you're able to speak freely. But try and make it quick. The machinery is all set up and ready to go. By tonight both of them will be nothing but a bad aftertaste, I guarantee it . . .'

There was a click as Tennant hung up. The girl from control switched off the tape recorder. 'That's all,' she said.

Dempsey looked at Makepeace. 'Did you see anyone hanging about when we left the Wilson house?' he asked.

'No, but I wasn't really looking for anyone,' she admitted.

'Neither was I. Shit! I take back what I said about Tennant. The guy is organized. I wish to hell we knew who was on the other end of that line.'

Makepeace frowned. 'I don't understand why the bug wasn't in the phone itself.'

'The car phone was fitted with a sophisticated anti-bugging device,' explained the girl. 'No way of nullifying it without making the phone unusable so we had to plant the bug in an ashtray in the rear of the front seat.'

'Isn't there a way you can get the number he punched by identifying the button tones?' Dempsey asked.

'We're trying that right now but there was a lot of distortion and background noise. We're running a copy of the tape through a series of filters. If we succeed, you'll be the first to know.'

'Good,' said Dempsey. He picked up the phone. 'Better warn the governor at Wormwood Scrubs that a murder attempt is going to be made on Wilson today.'

'At least we know the Chief is in a safe place,' said Makepeace.

The empty brandy glass fell from Spikings's fingers and landed on the thick carpet with a muffled thud.

'Sorry, sir,' he mumbled. 'Dropped ... your ... glass.'

The Commander came over to him. 'Gordon, you look terrible. I think you should take the rest of the day off and go home.'

'No ...' protested Spikings feebly. 'Just a bit dizzy. I'll be ... OK in a few minutes ...'

'Go home, Gordon. That's an order. You should never have been released from the hospital so soon, in my opinion.' He went back to his desk and pressed a button on the intercom. 'Marion, tell Jeffrey I want the Daimler right away. I'll be down immediately.'

Then he came and assisted Spikings out of the chair.

'Come on, we'll take you down the back way. Jeffrey will drive you home and in the meantime I'll call the department doctor and suggest he drop in and check you over . . .'

From the expression on Dempsey's face as he listened on the phone Makepeace knew something was very wrong.

'Transferred?' exclaimed Dempsey. 'Transferred to where?' While he waited for an answer he made a face at Makepeace. Then, 'What do you mean you don't know where? You must have some record! Where did the authority come from? That information's not immediately to hand either? What is this – Open Day at Wormwood Scrubs? Yeah, well, when you do find out call me back right away.' in the meantime could you at least tell me when Wilson checked out of your establishment?' Dempsey nodded and hung up.

'Wilson's gone,' he told Makepeace. 'And no one there seems to know where or why. He was taken away less than an hour ago.'

'Better tell Spikings right away,' said Makepeace. She picked up her phone and punched the Commander's extension number. His secretary, Marion, answered.

'I'm afraid the Chief Superintendent has already left,' said Marion after Makepeace had asked to speak to him.

'Back to his office or where?' asked Makepeace.

'Oh, he went home. He took ill in the Commander's office so the Commander sent him home in his own car. The Commander said he was probably suffering from delayed shock after that nasty business yesterday morning.'

'Put me through to the Commander. It's urgent,' ordered Makepeace, a chill spreading through her body.

'I'm afraid the Commander's on another line,' said
50

Marion apologetically. 'I imagine he's phoning for a doctor.'

Makepeace slammed the phone down and pulled open a desk drawer. She took out a Smith & Wesson .38 and shoved it into the special holster she had sewn into all her bras.

Dempsey needed no further urging to grab his own gun. 'What's up?' he asked, as he followed her out of the office.

'Spikings is out on the streets, unprotected apart from the Commander's driver. He's on his way home. Took sick in the Commander's office.'

They rushed out into the car park and then headed for Makepeace's Jaguar. 'I'll drive,' she told Dempsey. 'I know the quickest route to Islington from here. Let's hope we can get there before the Chief.'

'You figure that's where Tennant's goons will make their move?' asked Dempsey, as they got in the car.

'Where else? It's the one place they know he's got to go to sooner or later, especially since he only got out of hospital today. My bet is that they're either waiting in his flat already or are staked out around the building.'

She started up the engine and with a squeal of rubber the Jaguar sped out of the shop car park.

Dempsey took the .44 out of its shoulder holster and placed it on his lap.

It was as they were entering the New Kent Road that Dempsey spotted the Commander's Daimler up ahead. It was about fifty yards away. He pointed it out to Makepeace.

She nodded. 'I see it. I'll try and cut it off.'

But the traffic was heavy and Makepeace found it difficult to close the gap. They were still several cars behind the Daimler as they drove through the Elephant and Castle junction and on into London Road.

At the next set of traffic lights Makepeace drummed her fingers impatiently on the steering wheel.

'Take it easy,' said Dempsey. 'There's plenty of time.'

Makepeace frowned. 'What's that despatch rider up to?'

A motorbike courier, dressed in black leather and wearing an all-encompassing black helmet, had edged his powerful machine between the unmoving cars until he was level with the Daimler. He appeared to be talking to the Commander's driver.

'Probably asking directions,' suggested Dempsey.

The lights changed and the line of traffic began to more forward. 'Fuck,' said Makepeace.

Dempsey glanced at her in surprise. He had never heard her swear before. 'What's wrong?'

'They've turned in Lambeth Road instead of going up Blackfriars Road. Wherever they're going it's not Islington.'

'Maybe Spikings has got worse and the driver is taking him to a hospital.'

'Maybe . . .' said Dempsey as she followed the Daimler into Lambeth Road. She noticed that the despatch rider was keeping pace with the Commander's car. Then she noticed something else. 'Look!' she said, 'There's two of them now!'

Another motorbike rider, dressed in identical black leather, had joined the first one. They were flanking the Daimler like police outriders escorting an official car.

'I don't like this,' said Dempsey. He picked up the .44 and cocked it. 'Get closer.'

But then the Daimler turned again, this time into Kennington Road.

The lights turned red just as Makepeace reached the corner but she ignored them and sent the Jaguar wheeling round, narrowly avoiding a double-decker bus.

Ahead she saw the Daimler and its two sinister

shadows disappearing down a ramp that led into an underground car park.

'Hang on,' she warned Dempsey as she pushed hard on the accelerator. The Jaguar rocketed forward. Then there was a screech of tyres as she did a sharp turn into the entrance of the car park.

The gloomy, cavernous space was empty except for the Daimler and the two motorbikes. The Daimler was just coming to a halt at the far end and the two despatch riders were pulling up on either side of it.

Both the black-clad men turned as they heard the Jaguar scream into the car park. Makepeace glimpsed one of them pull something that looked like an oblong, black box from his jacket. There was a flicker of red flame and suddenly the windscreen went white. At the same time she felt something fizz past her left ear.

'Jesus!' cried Dempsey. 'A bloody machine-gun!'

Makepeace pulled violently on the wheel. The car swerved.

'I can't see anything!' she cried.

But Dempsey was already reaching forward to punch a hole through the frosted glass. The windshield shattered into powdery fragments, giving Makepeace a good view of the concrete pillar dead ahead.

The Jaguar ploughed into it.

CHAPTER EIGHT

'There goes my no claims bonus,' muttered Makepeace.

'You OK?' asked Dempsey.

'I'll check later . . .'

They both ducked as the machine-gun began its ominous chatter again. The windows on Dempsey's side exploded inwards, showering them with broken glass.

'Now what?' asked Makepeace, as she reached into her blouse and drew out the .38.

'Just get violent, Makepeace. Just get violent!'

Dempsey flung open his door and dived out. He hit the floor in a roll and came up firing. The Magnum sounded like a cannon going off, its boom echoing back and forth within the concrete confines of the car park.

The biker with the machine-gun was lifted from the saddle of his machine by the impact of the .44 bullet. Red gore blossomed out of the black leather covering his chest. He landed on his back behind his bike, the machine-gun clattering across the concrete floor.

His companion wheeled his bike around, gunned the engine and went hurtling towards the exit ramp.

Dempsey fired again but missed.

By now Makepeace was also out of the car. She had a better line of fire on the speeding bike rider and took advantage of it. Using a two-handed grip on her Smith & Wesson, arms extended, she took careful aim and pulled the trigger.

The biker was halfway up the ramp when his rear tyre exploded. The machine toppled over onto its side and skidded up the ramp for several yards in a shower of sparks. Its rider hit the ramp hard and rolled back down it.

'Nice shooting,' said Dempsey.

'From now on just call me Dirty Harriet.'

The bike rider lay groaning at the foot of the ramp. Dempsey hurried over towards him while Makepeace turned her attention to the Daimler. Jeffrey, the driver, was just getting out. His face was grey with shock. Makepeace ignored him. She wrenched open one of the rear doors. Spikings sat slumped in a corner, his eyes closed. He wasn't moving.

'Chief!' she cried, shaking him by the shoulder. 'Chief! Are you all right?'

Spikings's eyelids fluttered. Then he opened his eyes and looked at her. 'What are you after, Harry? A promotion?' he growled weakly.

Relieved, Makepeace helped him out of the car. He could hardly stand. 'I feel like I've been on the booze for a month,' he complained as he leaned against the side of the Daimler.

Jeffrey, still looking shocked, said, 'I had no choice . . . they made me come down here . . . One of them came up alongside me at the traffic lights and took out a gun . . . said he'd blow my head off if I didn't do as he said . . .'

'No one's blaming you,' said Makepeace, staring worriedly at Spikings, who was showing no signs of improvement.

Dempsey came over with the surviving bike rider. The latter's helmet had come off and he had an ugly gash down his right temple. He looked dazed and could hardly walk. Dempsey, with the barrel of the .44 shoved up against the side of his head, was practically carrying him.

'This guy is real eager to tell us everything he knows,' said Dempsey, giving him a push that sent him sprawling onto the floor. He ended up right beside his dead companion, who was now lying in a sizable pool of blood.

'Aren't you, bud?' asked Dempsey. 'Or do you want to join your pal here?'

Dempsey turned the dead man over with his foot. The .44 slug had gone straight through him, leaving an exit wound in the centre of his back at least four inches in diameter.

The surviving biker stared at the wound and swallowed. 'What do you want to know?' he muttered.

'Who do you work for?'

'Tennant.'

'And what were your orders for this little job?'

The man, in his late twenties and with the looks of a congenital yob, hesitated.

Dempsey cocked the Magnum and pointed it between his eyes. 'Well?'

'We were supposed to snuff him . . .' he pointed at the Commander's driver '. . . and take *him* to Tennant.' He pointed at Spikings. 'Preferably alive but it didn't matter if he wasn't.'

'And where were you going to take me?' asked Spikings, glaring at him.

'A building site . . . Not far from here. In Lambeth . . . Black Prince Road. The Stalwart Construction Company. Tennant owns it, I think . . .'

Dempsey said, 'Well, if Tennant's waiting for a delivery I think we'd better take the goods to him as planned. What do you say, Chief?'

Spikings nodded. 'Yeah. Let's do it.'

'You sure you feel up to it, sir?' asked Makepeace.

'No, but let's do it anyway.'

Dempsey bent down and picked up the discarded machine-gun. 'An Ingrams M10. Gonna be useful.' He holstered the Magnum and pulled the magazine out of the squat, ugly weapon. It was still half full.

He slammed the magazine back into the gun and

gestured with it at the biker. 'Okay, sweetheart, take off that macho outfit of yours.'

As the man began to remove his leather jacket and trousers Makepeace said, 'I get you – you're going to dress up in his gear.'

Dempsey shook his head. 'No. You are.'

'Me!' Why me?'

'For the simple fact that outfit is too small for me. On you it'll be a little big but no one's gonna have time to notice.'

'No. I refuse . . .'

'Do it, Makepeace,' ordered Spikings wearily.

She glanced down at the skirt she was wearing. 'But how can I . . . ?'

'Oh for God's sake, this is no time to be modest, girl. Just take it off!' snapped Spikings. 'And hurry up!'

Looking furious, Makepeace unzipped her skirt and stepped out of it. As quickly as she could she snatched up the black leather trousers and began to climb into them.

'Nice legs,' murmured Dempsey.

Makepeace turned on him. 'Just keep your bloody mouth shut!' she cried. 'Not one more word or else.'

Dempsey contrived to look innocent. 'I meant his,' he said, pointing at the biker.

She gave him a murderous look and picked up the leather jacket. 'I'm going to make you pay for this, Dempsey.' Then she sniffed, wrinkled her nose and groaned. 'Pew! And he's got B.O. on top of everything else.'

'Stop complaining, Makepeace,' said Dempsey. 'It's your vocation, remember?'

Charlie Wilson, his hands and feet cruelly bound with wire, was dumped unceremoniously into the three foot deep trench. At the end of the trench was a large cement-mixer truck, its drum slowly revolving.

There were four men standing around the trench. One of them was the bland-faced man who had switched briefcases with Spikings. He watched incuriously as Wilson struggled feebly at the bottom of the trench, then walked over to the Mercedes parked nearby. Tennant was sitting in the back.

'The others are behind schedule, Mr Tennant,' he said.

Tennant looked at his watch and said, 'Only by a few minutes, Moley lad. Give 'em time, give 'em time. Not everyone operates with your clockwork precision.' Tennant started to ease his bulk out of the car. The bland-faced man helped him.

Wheezing, Tennant walked over to the trench. By the time he reached it his fat round face was already covered in sweat and he regretted having to leave the air-conditioned comfort of the Mercedes.

He peered down at Wilson in the trench and said, with mock sadness, 'Goodbye, Charlie. Sorry it has to end this way but I'm sure you appreciate my position.'

'My kid . . .' gasped Wilson. 'What about my kid? You'll let him go now, won't you? You've got no reason to keep him now . . .'

Tennant sighed. 'Charlie, believe me there's nothing I'd like better than to let the little tyke go back to his mum but I can't take the risk. He's become a bit of an embarrassment too. Like father, like son, I suppose.'

Wilson writhed impotently in the trench. 'You fucking bastard!' he hissed.

Tennant went 'tsk tsk' then said, 'My advice to you, old son, is not to try and hold your breath when we start filling this hole. You'll only prolong the agony that way—'

'Mr Tennant!' called one of the men. 'The Daimler is just coming through the gate.'

'Good. That means Mr Wilson here will soon be joined by his sleeping partner. Open her up!'

Liquid concrete began to cascade out of the chute at

58

the rear of the truck. Wilson's struggles became more frantic but he was helpless to prevent the stuff from pouring over him.

Tennant watched the process with a satisfied smile then turned to greet the Daimler, which was pulling up beside his Mercedes. A rear door opened and Spikings was shoved out. He landed in the dirt on his face and knees. A black-clad figure wearing a helmet with a tinted visor got out behind Spikings.

'Ah, if it isn't Chief Superintendent Spikings, in the flesh!' exclaimed Tennant happily. 'You're just in time for my big cover-up.'

Spikings, still on the ground, said, 'Where's Wilson, Tennant?'

'Down there,' said Tennant, nodding towards the trench. 'Which is where you're going right now. OK Tom, or is it Dick?' he said to the leather-clad figure. 'Shove him in the hole.'

But instead of moving towards Spikings the figure reached up and removed its helmet. Tennant's mouth gaped open in surprise as he saw the blonde hair fall to the leather-covered shoulders.

'Actually my name isn't Tom or Dick. It's Harriet, but you can call me Harry if you like.'

For several seconds Tennant and his four men were too stunned to react. And by the time Tennant yelled, 'Kill her!' and started to reach for his gun it was too late . . .

Dempsey had come hurtling out of the front of the Daimler, the squat M10 spraying bullets at all five of them.

Tennant felt something tear into his lower stomach. He made a weak 'oof' sound and began to topple backwards. The next thing he knew he had landed on his back in the wet concrete with a loud squelch. It immediately covered his face. He struggled to sit up but he couldn't. His vast weight was pinning him down. He tried to scream as the viscous liquid poured into his nostrils and mouth . . .

Dempsey had the satisfaction of seeing all five of his targets drop as if pole-axed. He stopped firing and ran to the trench. A pair of fat, grey-covered arms protruded from the concrete, flailing about helplessly. Dempsey ignored them, jumped in the trench and began to probe the grey sludge with his hands. At the opposite end of the trench to where Tennant threshed about like a dying whale he found what he was looking for.

He hauled Charlie Wilson out of the trench and laid him out on the ground; then he cleared as much of the wet concrete as he could from his face. Wilson was choking and spluttering, trying to draw a breath.

Dempsey got his mouth open and succeeded in clearing his windpipe with his fingers. Wilson finally managed to breathe in.

After spitting out a large quantity of the liquid concrete, he gasped, 'My son . . . you've got to get him . . . please!'

CHAPTER NINE

Tessa, straddling Sean, was pumping her rangy andro-gynous body up and down violently on Sean's. It was stiflingly hot in the small bedroom and the sweat poured off both of them. Sean lay listlessly on the dirty mattress, the dark shadows under his eyes contrasting with the paleness of his face.

She stopped moving and stared down at him in disgust. 'Jesus, Sean, do I have to do all the bloody work?'

'I told you, I don't feel well,' he said. 'And my arm hurts worse than ever.'

'Bloody hell, you're useless!' She got off him and snatched up a packet of cigarettes. She lit one and puffed at it furiously while eyeing him with contempt.

'I need a doctor,' he complained, lifting up his bandaged arm.

'You need some balls, that's what you need,' she told him with a sneer. 'Look at you, as limp as a queer's wrist. Maybe I should go try Colin.'

'Colin? You'd screw him?' The idea had obviously shocked Sean out of his apathy, if only briefly.

'Why not?'

'But he's old. He must be forty at least.'

She shrugged. 'Probably a better man than you, though, especially right now . . .' She picked up her jeans and pulled them on, then, still bare chested, left the room.

'Hey, Tess!' called Sean. He started to sit up then fell back on the mattress and groaned.

Colin appeared not to notice Tessa's state of undress when she walked into the downstairs front room. He merely looked up from the old newspaper he was reading and said, 'How's Sean?'

'Depends what you mean,' she said sourly.

'His arm is what I mean.'

'That's useless too.'

She went and stood over the boy, who was sitting dejectedly in a corner, his knees drawn up under his chin. He stared up at her fearfully. She scared him in a way that the two men didn't.

'I can't wait to get shot of you, you little bastard,' she told him, then walked back to where Colin was sitting.

'Hot, isn't it?' she said, wiping the sweat from between her small breasts and flicking the drops at him with her fingers.

'You trying to tell me something?' Colin enquired blandly.

'What's it look like?'

'What about him?' Colin pointed a thumb at the ceiling.

'His battery's dead. I tried kick-starting him but no go,' said Tessa and gave a high-pitched giggle.

'I mean, won't he object?'

'Probably. So who gives a stuff? You?'

Colin shook his head.

'So come on then.' She unzipped her jeans.

'Hey, hold it,' said Colin. 'We can't do it in front of the kid.'

'Why not? Be an education for him. Not that he's going to be on this planet long enough to use it.'

Spikings surveyed the carnage and shook his head wonderingly. 'Dempsey, there should be a law against you.'

'There are probably several,' said Makepeace, thankfully removing the sweaty leather jacket.

Dempsey came back to the Daimler. 'Better call control and get the meat wagon out here. A couple of those guys are still breathing.'

'Tennant?'

'Think he's starting to set. You'd need a ten-ton crane to get him out of that trench now.'

While Dempsey used the radio in the Commander's car to call control Spikings, supported by Makepeace, walked over to where Wilson was sitting on the ground. Still covered in cement, Wilson was massaging his swollen wrists and ankles.

'That was a close one, Charlie,' Spikings told him.

'As close as I ever want to get. But what about my son? How are we going to find him?'

'Well, we can't ask Tennant now, that's for certain. One of these creeps might be able to tell us something if any of them ever regains consciousness but I don't want to wait that long. Luckily there's another option open to us.'

'What's that?' asked Makepeace.

But before Spikings could reply Dempsey joined them. 'Reinforcements are on the way,' he said, frowning, 'but there's something else. Something weird. Control think they've got the number that Tennant called on the tape but you'll never guess in a million years who it belongs to . . .'

'The Commander,' said Spikings calmly.

Dempsey and Makepeace stared at him in surprise.

'How did you know?' asked Makepeace.

'I've suspected it for a long time. Flushing him out was the difficult part though. It's taken a lot of work.'

Dempsey snapped his fingers. 'That explains why Tennant's bikers knew you were in the Commander's car.'

'And why they were on to you so quickly,' exclaimed Makepeace. 'You must have actually been in his office when Tennant phoned him.'

Spikings nodded. 'Then he slipped me a Mickey Finn in the brandy, sent me off in his car and called Tennant back.'

Dempsey hefted the M10. 'So let's go give him a surprise.'

'We'll give him a surprise all right but not the one you have in mind. Not yet at least,' said Spikings.

'Why wait?'

'Because first we want him to lead us to Charlie's son.'

'Detective Sergeant Dempsey is here to see you, sir,' said the Commander's secretary over the intercom. 'He says it's urgent.'

The Commander frowned. 'Send him in, Marion.'

The door opened and Dempsey entered. He looked unusually nervous and upset. 'Commander, we got ourselves a problem. A big one.'

'Oh really, Dempsey? What is it?'

Something the Chief was working on – a scheme to trap this hood called Tennant – it all went wrong.'

'How wrong?'

'Tennant's dead, but so is the Chief.'

The Commander's eyes widened in shock. Dempsey was impressed by the performance.

'Chief Superintendent Spikings is *dead*? He can't be! I sent him home only a short time ago. In my own car.'

'He was kidnapped on the way. By two of Tennant's guys. Your driver managed to alert us. Makepeace and I went after them. Traced them to a building site in Lambeth. There was a fight and I'm afraid the body count got kinda high. No survivors on Tennant's side.'

'No survivors,' repeated the Commander blankly.

'And a guy called Charlie Wilson went down the tube as well. Tennant had sprung him from prison somehow. By the time we got there Tennant had turned him into a foundation stone. Buried him alive in cement.'

'Good God!'

'It's a hell of a mess, sir. Nine dead bodies. Gonna take a lot of cleaning up.'

'I'll get on to the Chief Constable right away. In the meantime I want a full report from you and Makepeace.'

'We'll do our best, sir, but we don't have much of the background to the case. The Chief was playing the cards pretty close to his chest.'

'Nevertheless I'll need a detailed report,' said the Commander curtly. 'You're going to have to explain how it happened that all those people were killed, including the Chief Inspector. And needless to say I don't think any of this is going to reflect well on you, Dempsey. It seems to me that wherever you go large numbers of people get shot. This isn't New York, Dempsey. Your methods are too drastic for this city.'

'Yessir,' said Dempsey sullenly.

'Now go and start that report. After I've read it I'll speak to you again. And Makepeace too.'

Dempsey nodded and left. When he was gone the Commander sat looking thoughtful for several moments and then a wide, satisfied grin spread across his face. 'Well, Jack,' he murmured to himself. 'This is your lucky day.'

Dempsey went down to the car park and walked over to Tennant's Mercedes, which had been parked in a corner. Makepeace and Spikings were sitting in the back, concealed from sight by the tinted windows.

'Well?' demanded Spikings, who was beginning to look more like his normal self.

'Oscar-quality stuff. Very convincing.'

'So he bought it?'

'Oh yeah. He's probably working on the speech for your funeral right now.'

'Except that it's going to be him that'll be dead and buried before this day is out,' said Spikings grimly.

Tessa slammed the phone down angrily and looked at the other two. 'I don't understand it. There's no one at Tennant's place and no one at the Club's had any word from him all afternoon. He was supposed to call us here at one p.m. and it's four o'clock now.'

'What do you think's happened?' asked Sean nervously.'

'How the hell should I know? All I know is I don't like it,' snapped Tessa.

Colin said calmly, 'I think we should just sit tight and wait. Tennant won't let us down. The kid's too important to him.'

'I know that, idiot,' said Tessa, 'but I got the strong feeling something's gone wrong with his plans. And if he's in trouble so are we . . .'

There was a knock at the front door. Tessa grabbed a Mauser machine pistol from a nearby table. Colin was already on his feet and drawing a .45 automatic from his jacket behind the door. Sean just sat there looking confused.

'No one make a sound!' ordered Tessa in a fierce whisper. Then she pointed a warning finger at the boy huddled in the corner. 'One peep from you and I'll pull your tongue out.'

'Must be someone from Tennant,' whispered Colin. 'No one else knows that there's anyone in the place.'

'No one else did.' She edged her way to one of the front windows. 'There's a black cab out there. Driver looks as if he's waiting.'

The knocking at the door resumed.

'Someone should see who it is,' said Sean. It's got to be a message from Tennant.'

Tessa seemed to actually twitch with indecision. 'Shit,' she said finally. 'I'll go. Colin, cover me.' She shoved the Mauser down the back of her jeans and went into the passage.

She opened the door warily and stared at the balding, middle-aged man who stood outside. He seemed vaguely familiar.

'Who are you? What do you want?' she demanded.

'My name doesn't matter, Tessa. All you need to know is that I'm a friend of Tennant's,' said the Commander.

66

She frowned at him. 'I've seen you before,' she admitted. 'At the club.'

'Let's say I was Tennant's silent partner.'

'Was?' Tessa's body jerked as if she'd received an electric shock.

'Tennant's dead. I don't have time to explain the whole thing but I'm in charge now.' He took an envelope out from his jacket's inner pocket. 'There's cash in there, and an address for a safe flat in Kilburn. I suggest you go there right away.'

Tessa opened the envelope and looked inside. 'This isn't even a quarter of what Tennant promised,' she told him sourly.

'Just a downpayment. All I could get my hands on at short notice. But I promise you'll get double what Tennant offered. Just wait at the Kilburn place for me to contact you again. I'll arrange a trip abroad for all three of you.'

'What about the brat?'

The Commander's expression became pained. 'Wilson's dead too, so there's no reason to hang on to him.'

'If you want us to top him that's going to cost you extra.'

The Commander winced. 'I think it would be wise to, uh, get rid of him. You'll get an additional thousand pounds for the job. But don't do it here. Do it at the Kilburn place. It has a big garden out the back. Easier to dispose of the body.' He looked at his watch then said hastily, 'Got to go. I'll call you at the Kilburn address tonight.'

He hurried down the short, rubbish-strewn front path and got into the taxi. Tessa watched it pull away then she looked up and down the bleak Harlesden street. A few cars were parked around but nothing that looked suspicious. She closed the door.

Back in the front room she repeated the Commander's words to the others. Colin said nothing. Sean was

67

all for following the new instructions. 'Anything'd be better than staying here.'

'I agree,' said Tessa. 'But we're not going to Kilburn. It's a set-up. I don't trust him. He's trying to clean things up and that includes us. My bet is that there's someone waiting for us at Kilburn.'

'Cops?' asked Sean.

'No. Someone else. Someone who'll make sure we don't do any talking.'

Colin nodded. 'I think you're right.'

'So what do we do?' asked Sean.

'We get the hell out of London,' said Tessa. 'I've got friends down in Bristol we can stay with, while I figure out who that guy is and how we can screw everything we can out of him.' She turned and picked up a small leather bag. 'Go get the car, Sean. We're leaving right now.'

When Sean had gone Colin said, 'What are we going to do with him?' He pointed at the boy, who was staring at them fearfully.

Tessa was rummaging about in the leather bag. 'We can't take him with us. With Wilson dead his cow of a wife has probably told the police what happened by now. The brat's description will be everywhere.' She produced a fat, metal cylinder from the bag. 'Knew I had it somewhere,' she said as she fixed it over the end of the barrel of the machine pistol. Then she waved the silenced weapon at the boy.

'Stand up and turn around.'

He looked at the bulbous silencer, his eyes filling with tears. 'Are . . . you . . . going . . . to shoot . . . me?' he asked in a quavering voice.

'Smart little bugger, aren't you?' sneered Tessa. 'I said, stand up and turn around!' Her voice was like the crack of a whip.

Whimpering and shaking, Little Charlie got to his feet and slowly turned around.

Tessa aimed the gun at the back of his small head.

CHAPTER TEN

'Crazy Cat Four calling. The black cab is heading for the shop. Looks like the Commander is coming back to roost. Over.'

'Thank you, Crazy Cat Four. Over and Out.'

Makepeace switched off the radio. 'Any movement yet?' she asked Dempsey, who was peering out of the rear window. They were in a blue Ford Escort – one of the standard S.I.10 surveillance vehicles – parked some fifteen yards away from the house that the Commander had visited.

'Nope . . . no, wait! Front door's opening. Keep down! Someone's coming out. A young guy. Got a bandage on his right arm. Blood-stained. And he's coming this way . . .'

'What are you going to do?'

'Ad-lib,' said Dempsey, as he gently released the door handle.

When Sean was level with the car Dempsey kicked the door open. Sean made a grunting sound as the car door slammed into his stomach, knocking the air out of him. Even as his legs began to buckle Dempsey had grabbed him and was dragging him into the back of the car.

'My arm!' gasped Sean, as Dempsey pinned him to the seat with his knee.

'What's the matter with your arm, pal?' asked Dempsey, digging his knee into Sean's chest.

'Dog . . . bit it . . . chewed it up . . . bad . . . I need . . . a doctor . . .'

'You're going to need a priest by the time I'm through with you,' said Dempsey.

He clamped one hand over Sean's mouth and with

the other he began to squeeze the bandaged arm. Sean's eyes bulged and his body arched convulsively.

'Dempsey, really . . .' said Makepeace with distaste.

'Shut up,' he told her, as he squeezed Sean's arm even harder. 'In my book kidnapping kids is about the worst crime there is.'

Sean continued to buck and writhe under him. Dempsey released the arm several long seconds later and then removed his hand from his mouth.

Sean sucked in air and let out a rasping sob. 'Oh Jesus, don't touch my arm again . . . please! I'll do anything.'

'Glad to hear it. First you're going to tell me who else is in that house and what artillery they're carrying.'

Sean told him.

'Is the Wilson kid okay?'

'Uh, yeah, he's fine.'

'He'd better be,' said Dempsey. 'I find a mark on him I'm gonna grind your arm into hamburger and feed it to a large Briard I know.'

'How shall we play this, Dempsey?' asked Makepeace.

'We'll take this dick-brain to his car and have him drive it to the front of the house. When they come out we'll take them.'

'Going to be tricky with the boy in the way.'

'You'll hide in the back of the car – I'll get out the other side and double round. When they open the doors to get in we make our move. You grab for the kid while I come in from behind. We'll take them completely by surprise.'

'I hope you're right,' said Makepeace doubtfully.

Tessa's face was contorted with feral rage. 'For the last time, give me back that gun!' she hissed at Colin.

'And for the last time,' Colin told her stolidly, 'I'm telling you I don't hold with the killing of kids. We'll take him somewhere and dump him but alive, not dead.'

'It's too dangerous! He can identify us! He knows our names, you stupid bastard!' she spat at him. She was still rubbing her right wrist, which had been badly bruised when Colin had grabbed it and wrenched the machine pistol from her hand before she could shoot the boy.

'I don't care. I'm not going to be a part of killing a kid and that's final,' said Colin. He was holding both of the guns now. 'Besides, we'll be a long way away before the cops get any sense out of him. You can see for yourself he's scared shitless.'

At that moment they heard the hoot of a car's horn in front of the house.

'Jesus, what's Sean up to?' cried Tessa angrily. 'Why doesn't he sell tickets to the whole fucking neighbourhood!'

She went to the window and stared out. She saw Sean sitting in the battered Vauxhall Cavalier. He was looking anxiously towards the house.

Tessa sighed and her shoulders sagged. She turned to Colin. 'OK, you win. We'll take the kid with us and dump him. You wait and cover me while I take him out to the car.'

Colin nodded. 'Sure,' he said, relieved.

Tessa went over to the boy. 'Is the coast clear?' she asked Colin.

He went to the window. As he turned his back on her she picked up a kitchen chair and rushed at him. The chair shattered over his head just as he was turning back to confront her.

Stunned, he pitched forward onto his knees. Tessa tore the machine pistol from his weakened grasp. Then she turned its bulbous muzzle on him and shot him three times in the face. The silenced weapon made a sound like a large animal clearing its throat. Colin's

71

body shuddered and for a moment it seemed he was trying to stand up; then he fell forward and lay still.

Tessa looked down at him. 'Sorry Colin. You may have been a good fuck but you were also a stupid one.'

She turned her attention back to the boy who was trying to make himself invisible by hunching himself down as much as he could in the corner. 'I want my mummy,' he said in a tiny voice.

'Please kid, you'll make me puke,' she said as she aimed the gun at him.

'Tessa . . .'

She spun round. Sean was standing, swaying, in the doorway.

'Get back in the car, you cretin!' she cried. 'And keep your hand off the bloody horn.' Then she noticed how grey his face was and that there was blood dripping from the bandages on his arm.

'What happened to—' she began but before she could finish the question Sean was pushed from behind and sent staggering into the room.

Then a blonde woman stepped into view. She was holding a .38. 'Freeze!' she ordered Tessa.

Tessa merely grinned at Makepeace. 'My, you are a pretty one.' She raised the barrel of the Mauser.

'Drop the gun,' said Makepeace.

Tessa continued to grin. 'I didn't know the Brit cops recruited debs these days. What's your name, beautiful?'

'I'll count to five,' said Makepeace. 'If you haven't dropped that weapon I'll shoot you.'

'I'm afraid it's stalemate, beautiful. You shoot me and I'll riddle you with holes as I drop. One jerk on this trigger is all it will take, and it would be a pity to ruin that soft, expensive hide of yours.'

Sean, slumped against the wall, said, 'Tessa, I'm sorry. They made me . . .'

'Shut up,' she said, ignoring him. Her eyes, dancing

crazily, remained fixed on Makepeace. She seemed t
be enjoying the situation.

Makepeace realized she was facing a raving pyscho-
path. And the hate she could feel radiating from her
was almost palpable. She glanced at the boy. At least
he was still alive.

'So what are you going to do?' she asked Tessa.

'I'm going to back slowly until I'm within reach of
the kid and you're going to let me. When I have the
kid then we'll discuss terms—'

One of the front windows suddenly exploded
inward.

Tessa spun round and glimpsed a man aiming a
large revolver at her through the broken pane. She
opened fire with the Mauser. At the same moment she
felt something slam into her right side, knocking her
off balance. She looked and saw blood pouring out of
a hole between her ribs. Then she saw the smoke
coming from the barrel of Makepeace's .38.

'Bitch!' she screamed and swung the machine pistol
towards Makepeace.

There was a deafening boom and Tessa felt an impact
like the kick of a horse in her chest. She was only dimly
aware of being sent hurtling backwards through the
air. She hit the floor hard but there was very little
sensation. Soon there was no sensation at all.

Makepeace breathed a long sigh of relief and lowered
her gun. She looked at Dempsey in the window. 'You
OK?' she asked. She could see blood trickling down
his forehead.

'Yeah. Just nicked by a piece of glass. What about
you?'

'Apart from a pressing need to wring out my underwear I'm fine.'

He grinned at her. 'I'd be happy to handle your
laundry problems, princess.'

'Please. Not in front of the child.'

Makepeace went over to the boy and knelt down in

73

ont of him. 'Hello Charlie,' she said, smiling at him. 'You're safe now.' She reached out to touch him but he flinched away. She saw that he was staring, terrified, at her gun. She quickly holstered it and said, 'Hey, it's okay, Charlie. We're the good guys. We're going to take you home to your mum.'

Charlie's face screwed up and he started to cry. Makepeace hugged him. 'It's all right, Charlie,' she told him. 'It's all over now.'

Dempsey entered. After handcuffing Sean to a radiator and checking Tessa's body he joined Makepeace and the boy.

'Hey kid,' he said, hunkering down beside him. 'What's all this bawling for? Anyone'd think you'd been through a rough time.'

Charlie's crying eased up and he turned to look at Dempsey with wide eyes. 'You talk funny,' he said accusingly. 'Like the people on TV.'

Makepeace laughed. 'He's sure got your number, Dempsey.' To Charlie she said, 'Charlie, meet James Dempsey. He's from America. And you're right, he's just like what you've seen on TV – like Starsky and Hutch and their car all rolled into one.'

'Pay no attention to her, kid. She's kind of screwy. Been driving on the wrong side of the road too long.' He ruffled Charlie's hair. 'Come on, let's get you home to your mom. And there's a dog called Max who's kinda pining for you as well.'

The boy's eyes widened still further. 'You know about Max?'

'Sure. We're great pals.'

'They hit him. Is he all right?'

'A bump on his head, that's all,' said Dempsey, hoping that the Briard was still OK. It had been a nasty wound.

Makepeace stood up with Charlie in her arms. 'I'll take him home, Dempsey. You'd better call in the other

units and then go and see how the Chief is makir
out.'

'He said he wanted to handle it on his own.'

'Just the same I think you should check in on him.'

Dempsey shrugged. 'Whatever you say. You're the princess.'

The Commander was humming as he entered his office. But when the high-backed chair behind his desk swung round to reveal Spikings alive and well the sound died in his throat.

He came to an abrupt halt. 'Gordon . . .' he breathed.

'Just trying it on for size. The chair I mean,' said Spikings equably. 'Though perhaps you should be the one sitting down. All of a sudden you don't look well.'

'They told me . . . Dempsey said you were dead.'

'Reports of my death have been greatly exaggerated, Jack.'

'But . . .' He faltered, then staggered forward and leaned on the desk. His face had gone the colour of lead.

Spikings got up and quickly went to support him. 'Maybe the chair is a good idea, Jack, before you faint.' He helped him round the desk and sat him down.

The Commander took a deep breath. 'Gordon, what's this all about? Why did Dempsey lie to me?'

'Orders, Jack. From me.'

'But why?'

'Oh, stop it, Jack. It's all over for you. I know everything. Even the number of your Swiss bank account.'

'What?'

'When you heard that Tennant was dead you sent some people round to his house. But my lads got there first. Not only got all of Tennant's records but nabbed your lads when they arrived.'

The Commander was looking even more stricken. His mouth was working soundlessly.

'You and Tennant had a profitable little partnership all these years, didn't you? No wonder we could never pin anything on him with you protecting his back all the time.'

'But how did you find out it was me?' asked the Commander hoarsely. His voice sounded like it was coming out of a blocked drain.

'Oh, I've had my suspicions about you for years. Process of elimination. But I could never prove anything. So I decided to set up a time bomb that would shake you out of your tree like the rotten apple you are.' Spikings turned towards the door. 'Okay, you can come in now!' he called.

The door opened and Charlie Wilson entered.

'Meet my time-bomb. Charlie Wilson, ex-member of Tennant's gang, ex-convict but still an active member of S.I.10 . . .'

'What?'

'I took him on three years ago, without your knowledge, of course. He joined Tennant's gang and then we arranged for him to get himself nicked on that Christie's job. He was like a festering sore to Tennant ever since. I knew that when it finally seemed that he was going to spill the beans Tennant would over-react, and force you out into the open at the same time. Admittedly things nearly went very wrong – Tennant over-reacted in ways I didn't anticipate, but it all came out right in the end. For some people.'

The Commander sagged in the chair, then covered his face with his hands. 'I'm finished,' he moaned.

'You can say that again, Jack,' said Spikings. 'Now if you'd care to accompany us downstairs . . .'

'No, wait. Give me a few moments . . . a cigarette at least.' The Commander opened one of his desk drawers and produced a Smith & Wesson .38.

76

CHAPTER ELEVEN

Spikings gave the .38 in the Commander's hand a contemptuous glance. 'Give over, Jack,' he sighed. 'It's a waste of time. You're all washed up. There's nowhere for you to go.'

The Commander rose from behind his desk. 'I'm not going down without a fight, Gordon. I've got nearly two million dollars stashed away in Switzerland as well as several other smaller amounts seeded in different banks around the world. I'm not giving all that up – not after all those years of—'

'Hard graft?' suggested Spikings with a grim smile. 'Face it. You're in a hopeless situation. There's no way you'll be able to get out of the country.'

'Oh, I still have some contacts left. They'll help me to disappear. But first we're getting out of here. You two are coming with me. We'll use my private exit down to the car park. Move.' He waved the gun towards the exit door.

Wilson looked questioningly at Spikings.

'Better humour him,' said Spikings.

They walked to the door. Spikings opened it and ushered Wilson through, then followed him with the Commander close behind.

But as the Commander stepped through the doorway he felt the touch of cool metal against the side of his neck.

'End of the line, Commander. Freeze and drop it.'

The Commander glanced sideways and saw Dempsey with his back pressed against the wall, the .44 Magnum in his hand. He froze, but kept the .38 pointing at Spikings.

'I said, drop it, Commander,' said Dempsey coldly.

Remember what you said about my drastic methods and all? You know, that stuff about how large numbers of people get shot wherever I go?'

The Commander dropped his gun.

'But you were wrong about one thing, sir,' continued Dempsey. 'This place gets more like New York every day.'

At 3 p.m. that Friday Dempsey and Makepeace parked at the top of the hill in Greenwich Park, right next to the statue of General Woolfe.

As they got out of the car Makepeace said, 'This is a really nice gesture you're making, Dempsey. It comes as a major surprise to discover that beneath that callous, hard-boiled, brutal and ruthless exterior of yours there beats the heart of something almost human, give or take another million years of evolution.'

'Gee Makepeace, how is it when you pay me a compliment I still feel insulted?'

'I have no idea,' she said innocently.

Dempsey grunted and looked around the park. 'There they are,' he said, pointing.

Eileen and Charlie Wilson were walking slowly up the hill towards them with Little Charlie sitting on his father's shoulders.

'Hey there, Little Charlie! How ya doing?' called Dempsey.

Recognizing him, the boy waved excitedly. His father set him down and he ran up the hill.

'Seems to have made a speedy recovery from his ordeal,' said Makepeace quietly to Dempsey, as the boy approached them.

'Yeah, but I'll bet he'll have bad dreams for years to come . . .' Then, as the boy got close, he said, 'Hi, tiger! You're sure looking pretty happy. I guess you're glad to have your pop home again.'

'It's great!' Then a shadow passed across his face and

78

he said softly, 'But Max is . . . the vet had to put him to sleep . . .'

'I know, kid. I'm sorry. But I got someone here who might help you on that score.'

Dempsey walked back to his car and opened the rear door. A black puppy – a Briard – tumbled clumsily out onto the grass. The boy gave a gleeful cry and ran to it.

'His name is Harry,' Dempsey told him. 'After Miss Makepeace here. They both got the same sort of big, soppy eyes and they wag their tails the same way too.'

'How flattering,' said Makepeace.

By that time the boy's parents had arrived.

'Is that for Charlie?' asked Eileen.

'Sure is,' said Dempsey.

'You didn't have to . . .' said Charlie Wilson.

'Yeah, I did. But don't worry, I made Spikings pay. He also paid for all the pup's shots. Figured it was the least he could do after all he put you guys through.'

Wilson grinned. 'Well, he has given me a month's leave as well.'

'He's all heart,' said Makepeace. 'He's given us both a week's leave too. His promotion has gone to his head but I'm sure he'll be back to his usual self soon enough.'

'Yeah. Mean and ornery,' said Dempsey.

They all laughed and then watched Charlie and the puppy playing happily nearby.

Dempsey said, 'See, I was right, Makepeace. Harry wags his tail just like you . . .'

Later, as they were driving away from the park, she asked him how he was going to spend his leave.

'At the H20 Club, I hope,' he told her.

'You mentioned that place before. What's so special about it?'

'You can get a drink there anytime you want, for one thing. With the crazy licensing laws you've got in this country that means a lot to me.'

'Knowing you it's probably one of those seedy little clubs in Soho.'

'Hell no. It's a classy joint. You meet some pretty interesting people there.'

She nodded. 'Yes, I remember. The girl who sweats.'

'Nothing wrong with sweating, Makepeace. You should try it some time.'

'Humph.'

'So what are you going to do on your leave?'

'I was thinking of driving down to the country this weekend and visiting my father. I haven't seen him for ages.'

'Your old man is rolling in it, isn't he?'

'If "it" refers to money, no, he isn't. His taxes are outstripping his income. He's having to sell off parts of his beloved art collections just to stay afloat.'

'They valuable, these collections?'

'Very. One of them – a collection of antique jade pieces – is literally priceless.'

'So when he snuffs it you get to inherit all the loot?'

'Dempsey, please. That's my father you're talking about.'

'Hey, no offence. I'm just curious. I never had a millionairess for a partner before.'

'I'm not a millionairess.'

'Yeah, but you will be one day, providing your old man doesn't sell off all the good stuff in the meantime and stick you with the tax bills.'

'Really, Dempsey. My father would do no such thing.'

'You know, Makepeace, I wouldn't mind meeting your old man. I never met a real aristocrat before. How about you inviting me down to his mansion some time?'

'No offence, Dempsey,' said Makepeace coldly, 'But I really don't think you'd fit in there. And I'd hate for you to suffer any needless social embarrassment.'

*

'Your leave's cancelled,' growled Spikings.

'What!' cried Makepeace. 'But you promised . . .'

'Can't help that. Something's come up.'

'Something always comes up,' she said bitterly. 'It's not fair. I was just about to go out the door when you rang. I'd intended spending the week with my father.'

Spikings leaned back in the big chair. He had made himself at home in the Commander's office remarkably quickly. 'I know, Makepeace. And you can still visit him. But you'll be on duty.'

Makepeace frowned at him. 'I don't understand.'

'Your father obviously has friends in high places. Tell me, does the Prime Minister drop in for tea occasionally?'

Makepeace's frown deepened. 'Not to my knowledge, no.'

'You surprise me.'

'But certain members of the Royal Family do spend the occasional shooting weekend there.'

Spikings' eyes narrowed. 'Gordon Bennett,' he muttered.

'Why do you ask? What's all this about?'

'Your father is something of a collector, right?'

'Well, no, not really. It was my grandfather who was the collector. He was a true Victorian eccentric. On one occasion he travelled by camel all the way from the Sudan to . . .'

'Spare me the details,' said Spikings with a sigh. He glanced down at a sheet of paper on his desk. 'Your father has, in his possession, a collection of valuable Chinese jade artefacts, correct?'

'Actually they're part of a trust. Because of the taxes, capital gains, death duties and all that. As I was explaining to Dempsey only yesterday, my father—'

'They've been nicked.'

'Pardon?'

'I said they've been nicked. The lot. Happened in the early hours of this morning.'

'Good Lord,' breathed Makepeace. 'Poor Daddy.'

'Yeah, well "poor Daddy" is naturally very anxious to effect their recovery and has pulled some powerful strings to involve us – *you* in particular. I had some big nob from the Foreign Office on to me, among others. Apparently this jade collection is a politically sensitive issue.'

She nodded. 'Yes. The Chinese government have been demanding its return to China. They claim my grandfather stole it but, of course, that's—'

'Well, you'll be interested to learn that a representative from the Chinese government is staying with your father at the moment to discuss the problem. So you can imagine how embarrassing it is for all concerned, especially your father, that the collection should vanish at this precise point in time.'

'Yes,' she agreed. 'I can.'

'Especially since it appears to be an inside job.'

Makepeace gave a shocked gasp as the implications sunk in. 'You mean my father could come under suspicion?'

'Is under suspicion,' corrected Spikings. 'Which is why he's used his political pull to bring you – and us – into this thing. The sooner you recover the jade and nab whoever stole it the better it will be for your father. You've got four days and then it's a case for the Yard's art and antique squad . . .'

'But, sir,' she protested, 'the thief could be miles away by now.'

Spikings shook his head. 'Nope. The local police sealed off the whole area as soon as the alarm bell went off in their station. No one's left your father's estate since the robbery, according to them. So get moving, Makepeace.'

'Yessir.'

But just as she reached the door he said, 'Oh, and take Dempsey with you.'

She turned and looked at him aghast. 'Dempsey! You can't be serious, Chief.'

'Of course I'm serious. You'll need a back-up and he is your partner, so take him. Pass him off as your American boyfriend or something.'

'Pass him off as my *what*?'

'Look, Makepeace, your father's got a load of house-guests staying in that pile of his, so he wants you to carry out this investigation undercover as much as possible. So Dempsey will have to be passed off as a good friend of yours, if you get my meaning.'

Makepeace looked distressed. 'Dempsey – a guest in my father's home? I really don't think it's a good idea, sir.'

'Take him, Makepeace. That's an order.'

She straightened. 'Very well, sir. But I think you're asking me to do something over and beyond the call of duty, sir.'

He gave a dismissive wave of his hand. 'Just make sure he doesn't shoot anyone important.'

CHAPTER TWELVE

'So what do you do, Dempsey? I know now that was just a line you gave me about being in the oil business.'

Dempsey eyed the girl lying next to him in his bed, then sat up and reached for a cigarette. 'I'm a kind of trouble-shooter,' he told her.

'Oh yes? And what kind of trouble do you shoot?'

'All kinds.'

She reached up and ran her hand down his thickly muscled back. 'No, seriously. I want to know.'

'I'm a cop.'

'You're kidding.'

He shrugged.

'You're a Yank,' she said accusingly.

'So people keep telling me.'

'But you can't be a cop over here if you're an American.'

'It's not easy,' he admitted.

'You're teasing me. What do you really do?'

'I'm a hit man for the Mafia.'

'I thought so!' she exclaimed.

Dempsey laughed and rolled over on top of her, pinning her down with his weight. 'But this week I got no contracts at all . . . I'm a free agent.'

Her eyes shone with excitement. 'And I'm on holiday, which means . . .'

'Which means we got a whole week to get to know each other better,' he said, then pressed his mouth down on hers.

The phone started to ring.

Dempsey rolled off her and said, loudly, 'Shit!'

'Don't answer it.'

'I'm not going to.'

They both lay there listening to it ring. Finally Dempsey said, 'It's no good. I gotta pick it up.'

He reached over and answered it. 'Yeah?' he growled. Then, 'Jesus, Makepeace, you sure got a knack for calling me at inconvenient moments. What do you want?'

The girl watched in alarm as Dempsey's face went dark with anger. 'No way! Out of the question! I'm on leave! No, I don't care if it *is* orders, I'm not going anywhere!'

'Don't sulk, Dempsey,' said Makepeace.

'I'm not sulking,' he muttered.

'Yes you are. You've been sitting there seething away and glaring at the scenery ever since we left London. You're acting like a little boy who's lost his ice cream.'

'Makepeace, I am not in a good mood. Let's leave it at that, shall we?'

'Who was she, anyway?'

'Who?'

'Your ice cream. The one you were with when I called.'

'None of your business.'

'Not the sweaty one again?'

'Makepeace . . .' he said warningly.

'Look, it's not my fault,' she told him. 'It was Spikings' idea that you come along. I'm far from happy about the situation myself.'

'Yeah, I know. You're scared I'll embarrass you by eating with my fingers or something.'

'Oh, don't be silly. It's just that—'

'It's just that you're a snob.'

'I am not!' she protested.

'All you upper-class limeys are still snobs underneath the surface. That's one thing I've learnt since I've been in this screwy country. You still think you're living in the nineteenth century.'

85

'You don't know what you're talking about.'

'We'll see . . .'

At that point the Mercedes crested a low hill and Makepeace brought the car to a halt beside the road.

'There it is,' she said proudly. 'Winfield Hall.'

Dempsey stared at the walled estate that stretched out ahead of them. Dominating the scene at the end of a long tree-lined drive was a large, imposing-looking building.

'That the stately home your old man runs?'

'That's the stately home my father owns.'

'Some pile.'

'It dates back to the Restoration.'

'Restoration of what?'

She glanced at him, unsure if he was being serious or not, then started the engine again. As they headed down towards the main gates she said, 'My family have owned this estate since the time of the signing of the Magna Carta. You know what the Magna Carta is, don't you?'

'Yeah, of course I do. King Arthur and his knights and all that stuff.'

'Are you putting me on?' she asked, suspiciously.

'Princess, would I dare?'

Parked at the main gates was a police car. As they approached, a uniformed officer got out and signalled them to stop. Makepeace pulled up and wound down her window. The policeman peered in at her. 'Sorry, miss. You can't go in there without special permission,' he told her.

Makepeace produced her S.I.10 identification and showed it to him. 'It's all right, officer. We're expected.'

He reacted with surprise. 'Uh, yessir . . . I mean, ma'am, we were told you were coming but I didn't know that—'

'That one of us was a woman?' said Makepeace sweetly.

'Uh, no, sir, I didn't mean . . .'

'Ask him how soon they got the road blocks set up after the alarms went off,' interrupted Dempsey irritably.

Dempsey's American accent caused the officer to look even more confused. He opened his mouth to say something but then obviously changed his mind.

'Well?' asked Makepeace. 'You heard the question?'

'Uh, yessir, ma'am. We were here less than five minutes after we got the alert. No one could have got from the main house and on to this road in that time without us spotting the vehicle.'

'Couldn't the thief, or thieves, simply have climbed over the wall and got away on foot?' asked Makepeace.

'No, sir – I mean ma'am.' He shook his head firmly. 'We had men with dogs patrolling the perimeter of the estate less than ten minutes after the alarm. No one could have got away on foot in that time.'

'So in your opinion the jade, and whoever stole it, is still on the estate?'

'Yes, uh, ma'am?'

'Good. We'll let you know the moment we make an arrest,' said Makepeace and then, after giving him a nonchalant wave, drove through the gateway.

'You sure sound confident,' said Dempsey as they moved slowly along the winding drive.

'Oh, that was just to irritate the man. Honestly, what a male chauvinist pig! But then all the locals are like that out here. Talk about provincial.'

The Mercedes swept round a bend and the full imposing splendour of Winfield Hall, with its large ornamental lake in front, was revealed.

'Is the joint haunted?' Dempsey asked as Makepeace drove around the lake.

'Of course. By the ghost of a mysterious woman in black. She prowls the corridors in the east wing weeping her head off. No one has even been able to pin her down historically but her clothes are of the seventeenth century and she's obviously in mourning, so she's known as the Black Widow.'

Dempsey looked at her. 'You're kidding.'

'No, I'm not.'

'You ever see this ghost?'

'No,' she admitted. 'But I heard it several times when I was a child. And lots of people have seen it over the years. It was seen again only last year by one of my father's house-guests. Came into his bedroom and scared the life out of him. Who knows, Dempsey, you might be the lucky one this time.'

'Great,' he muttered.

She smiled at him. 'Don't tell me you're frightened of ghosts, Dempsey. I didn't think you were scared of anything.'

'I'm not scared of anything that lives and breathes, but ghosts . . . hell, ghosts are unnatural.'

'Well put,' she laughed. 'But don't worry – the Black Widow is harmless, so don't you go blasting away at her with your cannon if you should run into her. We don't want the family ghost dropping dead of a heart attack. Daddy would never forgive you.'

She brought the Mercedes to a halt right outside the main entrance. 'Leave your bag,' she told Dempsey as she got out. 'One of the servants will take care of it.'

'Servants too. I'm impressed.'

He followed her through the front door, which was unlocked, and into a small hallway.

'This way,' she said, and opened another door. This led into a truly baronial hall of daunting proportions.

'Wow,' said Dempsey, looking around.

A great, carved oak staircase led up to the rooms above and on the wall flanking the stairs hung large oil portraits of the Winfield ancestors. Suits of armour stood around in nooks fashioned out of the massive stone walls and at the far end of the hall was a long refectory table, with a minstrels' gallery above it.

'Wow,' said Dempsey again and walked over to a

suit of armour that stood near an ingle-nook fireplace, itself the size of a small room. 'Is this genuine?' he asked, tapping the helmet.

'Of course.'

'Hey, I've always wanted to wear one of these outfits. I guess in a previous life I must have been a knight in shining armour for real.'

'No, Dempsey, I think in a previous life you'd have been shining the armour at night.'

He gave her a pained look. 'See, I told you so! You consider me to be just a peasant. I was right. You're a snob, lady.'

'I was just jok—'

'Harry!'

A tall, elderly man had appeared in a nearby doorway. Dempsey saw the family resemblance immediately and wasn't surprised when Makepeace cried, 'Daddy!' and embraced him.

After hugging her, Lord Winfield held his daughter at arm's length and said, 'Let me look at you. It's been so long since I've seen you. Ah, you're as beautiful as ever. But pale. London air. Bad for you. You should spend more time up here. I've got a lot to tell you but first I want to hear about this appalling American hoodlum they've foisted on you — what's his name, Dimpsey? Dumpsey?'

Makepeace winced. 'Ah, Daddy, I'd like you to meet my colleague, Lieutenant James *Dempsey*.'

CHAPTER THIRTEEN

Lord Winfield didn't look embarrassed even momentarily. Without missing a beat he thrust his hand out towards Dempsey and cried, 'Pleased to meet you, young man! Why, you don't seem in the least bit appalling. I can't understand why Harry here was going on about you so. Perhaps she was referring to some other appalling American chappie.'

As he shook his hand Dempsey said dryly, 'Yeah, she probably was, Lord Winfield. There's a lot of us appalling Americans running about down at headquarters.'

Lord Winfield laughed. 'Call me Freddie, dear boy. Any friend of my daughter's is a friend of mine.'

Dempsey shot Makepeace an amused glance. 'What do you say, friend?'

Makepeace gave a pained smile and said to her father, 'Appearances to the contrary, Daddy, Lieutenant Dempsey is a very good detective. He's going to help me sort out this dreadful robbery business. In fact, it would be a good idea if we started on it right away.'

'Oh, but you've had such a long drive,' said Lord Winfield. 'Surely you'd like to relax with a drink first.'

'Yeah,' said Dempsey.

'No,' said Makepeace firmly. 'First you show us the scene of the crime and then we have the drink.'

Lord Winfield gave Dempsey an apologetic shrug. 'No use arguing with her, my boy.'

'I know,' said Dempsey.

The jade had been kept in a small anteroom. Apart from a steel and glass cabinet built literally into one of the walls it was bare of furnishings.

'This housed the collection,' said Lord Winfield,

indicating the cabinet. 'It was installed by the same firm that safeguard the Crown Jewels. Protected by all the latest gadgets . . .'

'You aren't kidding,' said Dempsey as he looked around, his trained eye detecting the various concealed devices. 'Infra-red beams, ambient temperature alarms . . .' He moved his foot over the carpet in front of the cabinet. 'And pressure pads. Impressive.'

'But none of them did the slightest scrap of good,' said Lord Winfield. 'Someone simply walked in here, tinkered the lock open and stole the lot.'

'What exactly did they take? I mean, what did the collection consist of?'

'Seventy-two pieces of jade, Mr Dempsey. Or, as we savants call it, nephrite. Every piece dating back to the Shang Yin Dynasty.'

'In other words, it's very old, Dempsey,' said Make-peace.

He ignored the sarcasm. 'How old?'

'The Shang Yin Dynasty lasted from around seven-teen sixty BC until the twelfth century BC,' said Lord Winfield.

'That is old,' agreed Dempsey. 'I'm beginning to see why it's so valuable.'

'It's priceless,' said Lord Winfield.

'Seventy-two pieces,' mused Dempsey. 'Can't be easy to hide that much jade. I guess the police have searched all the obvious places?'

'Oh yes. Frantic goings-on. Had them clambering about all over the place. Went everywhere, poking and prying. Taking fingerprints and all that.'

'No results?' asked Makepeace.

'The fingerprint experts told me they'd lifted thirty-three sets of prints. It turned out that twelve of those sets belonged to members of the constabulary.'

'And the rest? Who'd they belong to?'

'Well . . . myself, the staff and guests.'

'Were their rooms searched?' asked Dempsey.

'Thoroughly. All very embarrassing as far as the guests are concerned as you can imagine. Which is why I'd appreciate it if you could be as discreet as possible with your own investigation.'

'We'll try, sir. How many guests have you got staying?'

'Oh, eight in all.'

'They've been questioned?'

'Endlessly. The staff too.'

'I'd like details on all of them, if that can be arranged,' said Dempsey.

'Certainly,' said Lord Winfield. 'Come into my study and I'll have my secretary, Naismith, fetch the staff records down. The guests I can tell you about now.'

Lord Winfield led them into an attractive, oak-panelled room that smelled of leather and pipe tobacco. There were sporting trophies on display in two glass cases, racks of hunting rifles and shot-guns and several animal heads mounted on the walls, including that of a massive stag. But the thing that caught Dempsey's attention was the well-stocked bar at the far end of the study.

'Please help yourself,' said Lord Winfield, waving him towards it. 'And I'll have a dry martini. Very dry.'

While Lord Winfield picked up a phone and began talking Dempsey went behind the bar and got to work with relish. Makepeace leaned on the bar and watched him.

'You're quite an expert at that, aren't you?' she said, as he poured the ingredients into the cocktail shaker.

'It was a lady bartender from the Bronx who taught me all her tricks.'

'I bet she did.'

Lord Winfield hung up and came over to the bar. 'Naismith will be right down. Now what can I tell you about my guests?'

'For starters, just tell me who they are,' said Dempsey, handing him his martini.

'Well . . .' he paused and looked with surprise at the glass. 'I say, this is very good!'

'Thanks.'

Makepeace said, 'Well, at least you've got a profession to fall back on, Dempsey, when they take away your badge. You can open your own bar.'

He narrowed his eyes at her. 'And what can I fix for you, sweetheart?'

'I'll have a Pimms. With lots of ice.'

Lord Winfield drained his glass and said, 'Now where was I? Ah, yes, my guests. There are three married couples – there's Biffin and his wife, Esmeralda. Both old friends of mine. Above reproach and all that. Besides, Biffin's suffering from a slipped disc . . . Then there's Selwyn and Prunella. Selwyn turned up late. Had to attend a committee meeting at the House of Lords. He only arrived this afternoon. Prunella drove down last night with an American couple, Andrew and Susan Sims . . .'

'American? Do you know them?' asked Dempsey.

'No. Never met them before. Selwyn ran into them at some London function last week, took a shine and suggested they come for the pheasant shoot. Apparently Andrew fancies himself with a gun. Squirrel's eye at six hundred paces and all that. He'll probably wear a coonskin hat for the shoot.'

'How do you read him?'

'Andrew? Oh, seems a nice enough feller. Talks a lot, and loudly, but then you Americans always do, eh?' Lord Winfield grinned mischievously at Dempsey.

'No, Daddy, Dempsey here is one of the strong, silent types,' said Makepeace.

Dempsey sighed. 'What's this Andrew guy do for a living?'

'He's in oil, I believe.'

'Small world,' muttered Dempsey.

'Pardon?' asked Lord Winfield.

'Nothing. Who else is there?'

'Ah, that just leaves Frances Trafford, a dear friend of mine. Sad business actually, she still hasn't recovered from the death of her husband, Dick – another old friend of mine – and that was a year and a half ago. And, of course, the gentleman from the Chinese Embassy, a Mr Ch'ien Cheng Tsu. And I hardly think you could suspect him of the robbery.'

'Why not?' asked Dempsey. 'Perhaps the Chinese have decided to just grab the jade instead of politely waiting for it to be handed over.'

'Highly unlikely, dear boy. Because this latest bout of negotiations has been going very much in their favour. I'm under a great deal of pressure from our government to comply with the new Chinese proposal regarding the jade. Mr Ch'ien Cheng Tsu is well aware of this so it's doubtful he would jeopardise the situation with such a rash act.'

'I see,' said Dempsey thoughtfully. He finished the large bourbon he'd poured for himself and looked Lord Winfield straight in the eye.

'That brings us to you, sir. From what you've just told me it seems that you have the best motive of all for taking the jade.'

'Dempsey!' cried Makepeace, shocked.

Lord Winfield held up a hand. 'No, darling, he's quite right. It does look bad for me, I admit. Which is why I hope you can sort out this mess before I disappear under a ton of circumstantial evidence. You've got to clear the family name, Harry old dear.'

There was a knock on the door. Lord Winfield called 'Come in!' and a man entered. He was in his late thirties and dressed entirely in black. The darkness of his clothing accentuated the whiteness of his skin, which had an unhealthy tinge to it. His black hair was slicked back from his high forehead and highlights glittered on the thick layer of oil covering it.

He approached Lord Winfield in a blatantly obsequious manner, carrying a small stack of cardboard folders. 'My Lord, the staff files as you requested.'

When he'd handed them to Lord Winfield he turned to Makepeace. 'Miss Harriet, how delightful to see you back.'

'Hello, Naismith,' said Makepeace without enthusiasm.

He turned to Dempsey and raised an enquiring eyebrow.

'Uh, this is . . . Mr Dempsey,' said Makepeace. 'He's a . . . uh, a friend of mine. He'll be staying here for a few days.'

Naismith inclined his head a fraction of an inch towards Dempsey. 'A pleasure, sir. I trust you will enjoy your visit.' Then he turned back to Lord Winfield. 'Will that be all, sir?'

'Thank you, Naismith.'

'Very good, my Lord.' He turned and nodded at Makepeace and Dempsey. 'Miss Harriet, Mr Dempsey.' Then he glided out of the room.

When the door had closed behind him Dempsey said, 'Jesus, is that guy for real?'

'I know what you mean,' said Makepeace. 'He makes my flesh crawl.'

'Now, Harry, don't start that again,' said her father. 'Naismith is a very efficient secretary. I'd be lost without him.'

'He's oily. Oily and unctuous,' she insisted.

'Oily?' said Dempsey. 'The guy's got more oil on his head than there is under Texas.'

Makepeace laughed. Lord Winfield frowned and passed the folders to Dempsey. 'All the details on my employees. But I'm positive none of them are involved. They've all been with the family for years. I know and trust every one of them.'

'How long has Naismith worked for you?'

'Ah, well, yes, he is a relative newcomer. He's only

95

been with me for three years. But I did know his father. Used to be my batman in the army.'

Dempsey was looking through the folders. 'His file isn't here.'

'Isn't it? He must have overlooked it. I'll speak to him later and get it for you.'

'Thanks. So when do I get to meet these guests of yours?'

Lord Winfield looked at his watch. 'We're having pre-dinner drinks in the rose garden, seeing as it's such a warm evening. That'll be in an hour from now. You can meet everyone then. In the meantime perhaps you'd care to get settled into your room? Harry will show you the way.' He turned to Makepeace. 'You'd better check with Mrs Bates first but I'm sure that all of the guest-rooms in the east wing have been made up and are available.'

'The east wing? Isn't that where your ghost hangs out?' asked Dempsey.

Lord Winfield raised his eyebrows. 'You've heard about our ghost?'

'Yeah. Your daughter was spinning me a line about it on the way here. I figure it's a family joke, right?'

'Oh no, James, on the contrary. The Black Widow is quite real. Why, I saw her in the east wing only a month ago.'

Dempsey looked at Lord Winfield and saw that he appeared to be completely serious. He poured himself another Bourbon and muttered, 'Are you sure you haven't got a spare room in the west wing?'

CHAPTER FOURTEEN

There was a knock at Dempsey's door. He got up from the four-poster bed on which he'd been stretched out and went to the door. He opened it and blinked with surprise. Makepeace was standing there in a blue evening gown that was cut remarkably low.

Surveying her *décolletage* with obvious pleasure he exclaimed, 'Makepeace, this is a side of you I've never seen before!'

She immediately folded her arms over her chest. 'Is it safe for me to come in or should I go fetch a whip and a chair?'

He stood aside. 'Enter, princess. If it'll make you feel better you can have my gun. I can see you're not packing your own in that outfit.'

She swept into the room and looked around. 'Is the accommodation up to your standards, Dempsey?'

'It's neat. Like something out of a movie. I was just test-driving the bed. Wanna go for a drive around the block with me?'

'I'll pretend I didn't hear that. It's time we joined the others in the rose garden. Are you ready?'

He looked at her dress. 'Is this event formal or what?'

'I'm afraid so. I should have warned you to pack your dinner suit before we came up here.'

'I don't have one,' he told her as he put on his sports jacket.

She eyed it critically. 'Perhaps Daddy has one that will fit you. I'll ask him . . .'

'Don't bother. I'm not dressing up like a penguin just to have a couple of drinks in the back yard.'

'As long as you won't feel embarrassed.'

'Me? You're kidding.'

'Even a skin as thick as yours must have a few chinks in it, Dempsey.'

'The only chink around here is the guy from the Chinese Embassy.'

Makepeace groaned.

The other guests were already in the rose garden when Dempsey and Makepeace emerged from the house. Elegantly attired, they stood about sipping champagne amid the splendour of the impeccably landscaped surroundings. Servants moved among them with trays of canapés and fresh glasses of champagne. On the side-lines stood Naismith, keeping a supervisory eye on the servants.

Dempsey was impressed. 'It's like a scene out of a movie,' he murmured to Makepeace.

'Your highest form of praise,' she replied dryly.

Lord Winfield hurried towards them. 'Ah, Harry, you look splendid! Marvellous! The spitting image of your dear mother in that gown.' Then he turned to Dempsey, glanced at his casual dress and raised an eyebrow.

'You'll have to make allowances for Dempsey, Daddy,' said Makepeace hurriedly. 'Once a plain-clothes man, always a plain-clothes man.'

'Uh, yes. Well, come and meet everyone.'

Lord Winfield led them across the lawn towards the other guests.

As they approached a tall, black-haired woman standing alone Lord Winfield said to Dempsey in a stage whisper, 'Frances Stafford. The one who lost her husband. He was an archaeologist. Died of some dreadful disease in the Far East.'

Aloud, he said, 'Frances, my darling, what are you doing here all alone? Why aren't you mingling?'

As Frances Stafford turned Dempsey saw that she was still a very attractive woman with striking cheekbones that set off her large green eyes. Her mouth was wide and sensual and the gown she was wearing revealed a body that was slim and lithe. But Dempsey noticed the bruised, puffy areas under her eyes – the tell-tale signs of a heavy drinker.

'Hello, Freddie. And Harriet! It's been ages . . .' Then she looked, with obvious interest, at Dempsey. 'And who is this?'

'This is James Dempsey. From America. He's uh, here with Harry,' said Lord Winfield.

'Pleased to meet you, James Dempsey from America,' she said in a sultry voice, extending her hand to him. Then she gave Makepeace an amused smile and said, 'I must say I admire your taste in men, Harriet dear.'

Makepeace smiled weakly.

As they moved away Dempsey muttered to Makepeace, 'That's the grieving widow?'

'Yes. What did you think?'

'Wow.'

'I mean as a suspect.'

'I'd have to carry out a more intensive interrogation before I come to any definite conclusion.'

'I can imagine the form it would take.'

'You're just jealous.'

By now they were approaching a couple in their early thirties. They could have been brother and sister; both were handsome and bronzed, with the same blond hair. The man's muscular build was clearly visible through his dinner suit and the woman had the body of a trained athlete.

'Andrew and Susan Sims,' announced Lord Winfield. 'Fellow countrymen of yours, James.' He turned to the couple. 'My daughter's boyfriend here is from America too,' he explained. Makepeace winced at the word boyfriend.

'Yeah?' said Andrew Sims, grabbing Dempsey's hand and subjecting it to a bone-crushing grip. 'Whereabouts do you hail from, Jim?'

99

'New York,' said Dempsey, not letting the pain show on his face. 'What about you, Andy?'

'Chicago, originally. But now we're based in Houston. Great town. We love it there, don't we baby?' He turned to his wife.

She nodded enthusiastically. 'It's a great little town. What are you doing in England, Mr Dempsey?'

'Oh, I'm on a sort of combined vacation and business trip,' he said, accepting a glass of champagne from a waiter.

'What line of business are you in?' asked Andrew Sims, staring intently at him.

Before Dempsey could answer, Makepeace said quickly, 'James is a writer. He's over here doing research on a new book.'

'What about?' asked Susan.

Dempsey looked at Makepeace. 'You can tell them, sweetheart. I don't mind,' he said, then sipped his champagne.

Makepeace paused for only a fraction of a second. 'It's about the London underworld and its connections with organised crime in America. Uh, that's how we met. I was assigned to give him a guided tour around some of the less salubrious parts of the East End.'

Andrew Sims switched his intense gaze to her. 'Oh yeah, that's right. Lord Winfield mentioned you were a lady cop . . .'

'My daughter has the bizarre ambition to become the first female Commissioner for the Metropolitan Police,' said Lord Winfield, not without a hint of pride in his voice.

'We've sure seen a hell of a lot of cops today,' said Sims. 'You joining in the hunt for the missing jade too?'

Makepeace shook her head. 'No, this is a social visit only. Besides, I'm way out of my jurisdiction.'

Lord Winfield took hold of her elbow. 'You must come and say hello to Biffin and Esmerelda. It's been

100

so long since they've seen you. Excuse us, Andrew . . .
Susan . . .'

Dempsey nodded to the couple and followed Makepeace and her father across the lawn towards an
unlikely looking trio. It consisted of a red-faced cari-
cature of an old-fashioned British army major, a regal-
looking woman who was obviously his wife and a
short, thick-set oriental man wearing a black Mao-style
jacket. The latter, Dempsey realized, had to be the jade
negotiator from the Chinese Embassy.

Dempsey stood impassively by while Biffin and
Esmerelda made effusive sounds at Makepeace. Then
Lord Winfield remembered his presence and intro-
duced him to the Chinese official.

'This is Mr Ch'ien Cheng Tsu. Mr Ch'ien, James
Dempsey from America. He's uh, a writer.'

Dempsey shook Ch'ien's hand, noting the hidden
power of his grip and the hardness of his skin. He also
took note of the bulge of muscle beneath Ch'ien's
expensive and impeccably cut Mao jacket. Dempsey
decided he was no ordinary diplomat.

'I am pleased to meet you, Mr Dempsey,' said Ch'ien,
in a low, well-modulated voice containing hardly a
trace of accent. His age could have been anything
between thirty and fifty.

'Same here,' said Dempsey. 'You sure speak good
English, Mr Ch'ien. I guess you've been stationed at
your embassy here for quite a time.'

'On the contrary, Mr Dempsey, I am not part of the
permanent contingent at our London embassy. I am
only visiting the country. As soon as my business here
is completed I shall be returning to China.'

Dempsey nodded. 'Lord Winfield told me about the
jade negotiations. But it looks like your visit may be
an indefinite one if the stuff isn't found.'

'Oh, I'm sure it will be located soon, Mr Dempsey. I
have great faith in the methods of your Western police

forces.' As he said that he gave a polite smile. Dempsey couldn't tell if he was being ironic or not.

They made inconsequential small-talk for a few minutes and then Lord Winfield took Dempsey aside to introduce him to the final couple, Selwyn and Prunella King. Selwyn had the haughty looks of an aging head-waiter, while his wife reminded Dempsey of a horse that had seen better days. She even had a braying laugh to go with the elongated, toothy face.

Dempsey was relieved when Makepeace extracted him from their company and had him stroll with her to the other side of the garden.

'Well,' she said, when they were out of earshot of the others, 'what do you think?'

He told her of his impression of Ch'ien and then said, 'Tell me about the two you just rescued me from. He's the politician?'

'Ex-politician. He lost interest after they banished him up to the House of Lords. Prunella's still ambitious on his behalf, according to my father, but they're as poor as church mice.'

'That's interesting. What about the other couple?'

'Biffin and Esmerelda? Oh, they're rolling in money so I think you can safely cross them off your list of suspects.'

'Maybe. Old Biffin looks like he led the Charge of the Light Brigade. Ex-army?'

'Yes,' nodded Makepeace. 'He may look like an old buffer but he was a very brave soldier in his time. Won the Military Cross.'

'Yeah? For what?'

'Oh, some act of heroism back during the Korean War.'

'There it is again.'

'What?'

'The oriental connection.'

'What connection?'

'Frances Trafford lost her husband in the Far East,

102

we got Mr Ch'ien from China and now you tell me ol' Biff saw action in Korea. That's what I call a connection.'

'That's what I call a coincidence,' said Makepeace.

'More champagne, madam, sir?'

They both turned round, surprised. Naismith was standing directly behind them, holding a tray. Neither of them had heard his approach.

Dempsey gave him a cold look but took another drink anyway. Makepeace took one too. 'Thank you, Naismith.'

Naismith didn't leave. 'Uh, Miss Harriet, will your guest be taking part in tomorrow morning's shoot? I need to know this evening. To inform the gamekeeper and so forth . . .'

Makepeace looked inquiringly at Dempsey. 'Will you?'

'What will you be shooting?'

'Pheasants, of course.'

Dempsey shook his head. 'Doesn't sound like my kind of scene, shooting overgrown chickens. I prefer bigger game. But I'll watch if that's okay.'

Lord Winfield's secretary winced slightly and said, in any icy tone, 'I'm sure no one will have any objection, sir.'

As Naismith glided back across the lawn Dempsey muttered, 'I expect to see him leaving a trail of oily footprints behind. That guy is slimier than a bucketful of snails.'

'I know what you mean. But I'm surprised you're not joining the shoot, Dempsey. I would have expected it to be exactly your cup of tea.'

'Like I told the human oil-can, I prefer bigger game. And I got a strong suspicion I'm gonna flush it out before the weekend is over.'

*

103

When Dempsey finally got back to his room that night he had made only one conclusive discovery – that the British aristocracy could put the booze away faster and in greater quantities than a platoon of U.S. marines on a weekend pass. Even he had had trouble in keeping up and was now actually feeling a little unsteady on his feet as he made his way to the four-poster bed.

He contemplated reading through the stack of employee's files on the table beside the bed but decided the chore could wait until the morning. Instead he stripped, turned off the light and slipped naked between the smooth sheets.

He was almost asleep when he heard a sound in the passageway outside. He realized it was a woman crying. Then he heard a soft tapping at his door.

Puzzled and half asleep, Dempsey got out of bed and pulled on his pants. He was halfway to the door when he remembered the ghost . . .

He froze for a few seconds, suddenly wide awake. Then he told himself he was being an idiot and continued to the door.

He switched on the light and opened the door. But there was no one there.

He stepped out into the corridor and looked up and down it. Suddenly, out of the shadows, a shape materialized. It was a woman. She was dressed in black and had long, black, flowing hair but her face was so pale it seemed to glow in the dark.

Dempsey felt cold fingers of atavistic terror go dancing up his spine. He wanted to move but he couldn't. He could only stand there helplessly as the ghost of Winfield Hall came straight at him . . .

CHAPTER FIFTEEN

As soon as the apparition in black flung its arms about him Dempsey knew he was dealing with a live woman and not a ghost. Ghosts didn't have warm flesh. Nor did the average ghost smell of brandy fumes.

It was Frances Trafford and she was very drunk.

'James, quickly!' she said urgently. 'Back inside! Before he finds out . . .'

She shoved him backwards into the room and then hurriedly shut the door. She leaned her back against it and closed her eyes. She was breathing rapidly and the plunging front of her black nightdress provided Dempsey with clear proof that she was a very well-developed woman.

Dempsey still hadn't fully recovered from the shock she'd given him in the corridor. He stared at her in confusion. 'Who's *he*?' he asked her. 'And what are you doing here?'

She opened her eyes but had obvious difficulty focusing on him. He was surprised she was still capable of standing up. 'I can't tell you his name – it's best you don't know anything about all this,' she said, her voice slurred. 'As for what I'm doing here – surely that's quite plain . . .'

She then reached up and pulled the straps of her nightdress off her shoulders. Suddenly she was naked all the way down to her hips. Then, slowly, the nightdress slid the rest of the way to the floor, forming a dark pool of silk around her feet.

Dempsey looked at her long, white body and swallowed hard. Tearing his gaze away from her rapidly rising and falling breasts, which would have been equally impressive in repose, he said, 'Look, lady, don't think I'm not flattered by the offer but I honestly feel that you're in no shape to last the distance . . .'

'Shape? What's the matter with my shape?' She pushed herself away from the door and lurched towards him. He stepped quickly forward and caught her just as she started to stumble.

As they clung together Dempsey became aware of two things: that her nipples were hard and erect against his bare chest, and that the brandy fumes on her breath were so strong they were making his eyes water. Even as he felt his desire for her begin to increase he knew his initial reading of the situation was correct: she was so drunk she would be useless in bed.

'Where is she, anyway?' she asked suddenly, peering suspiciously about the room.

'She? I thought you were worried about a he.'

'I'm not talking about *him*. I'm talking about Harriet. I was afraid she'd be here. Why isn't she?'

'Why should she be?'

'You're her lover, are you not? That's the impression Freddie was giving. I must say I was surprised to see Miss Goody-Two-Shoes turn up with a hunk like you. Wimps are usually more her style. I've always suspected she was frigid. I thought that was the reason her husband — that solicitor — left her. Is she frigid?'

'Not that I've noticed,' said Dempsey, wondering what the hell to do with her.

'Then why isn't she here with you?'

Dempsey thought quickly. 'She didn't want to upset her father. She told me he had pretty old-fashioned views about that kind of thing.'

'*Freddie*? Don't make me laugh. He's a randy old bastard. So what's the real reason Snow White isn't here having those policewoman brains of hers screwed out by you? Is she insane or what?'

He had no answer for that one. While he was trying to think of one she disengaged herself from his arms

106

and staggered across to his bed. She flopped down onto it and then rolled over on her back.

'Come on, hurry up,' she moaned, 'and for God's sake don't be gentle with me . . .'

Dempsey stood there undecidedly. He had to admit he was tempted. Frances Trafford stretched out on his bed like that made an arousing sight but he just didn't feel right about making love to someone who was so drunk.

Reluctantly he said, 'Mrs Trafford, I really think it would be wiser if you let me help you back to your room.'

There was no reply.

'Mrs Trafford?' He moved closer to the bed.

She started to make an odd noise. With a start he realized she was snoring. She was out cold.

'Shit,' he muttered. He sighed, bent down, pulled the bedcovers out from under her, then covered her with them. She stirred but didn't wake up.

As he stood looking at her he contemplated getting into the bed with her but decided that this might not be a wise move. She was quite likely to wake up in an alcoholic blank, find she was lying next to a strange man and start screaming the place down.

So he turned the light off and went and stretched out in one of the large leather armchairs.

'This knight-in-shining-armour crap is catching,' he muttered to himself as he drifted off to sleep.

Dempsey headed towards the shooting party that was strung out in a rough line across the moor. He wasn't feeling very well. He had a hangover and a neck-ache from sleeping in the armchair.

As he got closer to the line of shooters he recognised Makepeace. She was standing with her father and a man Dempsey hadn't seen before.

'Morning, James,' said Makepeace as he joined them.

107

'I was beginning to wonder what had happened to you, you weren't at breakfast.'

Makepeace was looking every inch the country lady. She was wearing a tweed skirt, a hacking jacket and expensive boots. She was also holding a shotgun in a way that suggested she'd been born with it in her hands.

'I overslept,' he told her and nodded a greeting to Lord Winfield.

Lord Winfield introduced him to the other man, who was heavily built and had the complexion of someone who spends most of his time outdoors. 'This is Jessop. My estate manager. Jessop, Mr James Dempsey.'

Dempsey shook Jessop's calloused hand. 'Not shooting, Mr Dempsey?' Jessop asked him.

'No. Guns are out of my line,' he said, uncomfortably aware of the weight of the .44 Magnum under his left shoulder. 'Harriet, sweetheart, mind if I have a few words with you,' he asked Makepeace.

She glanced questioningly at her father. He looked at his watch. 'Should be a couple of minutes before the beaters have the birds breaking cover in this direction. Right, Jessop?'

The burly estate manager nodded. So Makepeace followed Dempsey several yards back behind the line.

'What's up?' she asked him when they were out of earshot.

'I had a visitor last night. A lady in black.'

'You're joking! You mean you actually saw the Black Widow?'

'I saw *a* black widow,' he told her and indicated the distinctive figure of Frances Trafford who was standing some distance down the line.

Makepeace raised an eyebrow. 'You intrigue me. What happened?'

'Very little. She made a pass at me and then passed out colder than a dead mackerel.'

'So what did you do?'

108

'Put her to bed and bunked down in an armchair. As a result my neck feels like someone tried to turn it into a pretzel.'

Makepeace regarded him suspiciously. 'And then?'

'And then what?'

'And then what indeed.'

Dempsey frowned. 'I don't get you.'

'What happened this morning? When the dead mackerel returned to life.'

'She was gone when I woke up. I didn't even hear her go. She must have had second thoughts about me when she'd sobered up.'

'I'm not surprised.'

'Anyway, the important thing is that she was scared of some guy. She said she was scared *he* would find out . . .'

'And you don't know who he is?'

'She wouldn't say. I thought you might have some idea. Is there anyone staying at the house who she's been knocking around with since her old man kicked the bucket?'

'No one that I know of. I can't imagine that any of the male guests fit the bill – it's hardly likely to be Biffin or Selwyn. And Andrew Sims is a newcomer . . .'

'One of the staff, maybe?'

Makepeace looked faintly shocked. 'I hardly think so.'

After a pause, Dempsey said, 'What about your father?'

Makepeace now looked very shocked. 'Have you lost your mind?'

'Frances called him a randy old bastard. Could be she was speaking from first-hand experience.'

Her face had started to go bright red. 'I've never heard such rot in all my life!'

'Hey, sorry, princess, but I got to consider all the possibilities. Your problem is you're too close to the situation.'

Before she could reply the still morning air was

shattered by the sound of a shotgun being fired. The birds had obviously arrived.

Giving Dempsey a final, furious glance Makepeace turned and hurried back to join her father on the shooting line.

The gunfire grew in intensity as more pheasants, driven by the beaters, came heading towards the line of shooters.

Dempsey watched as a curious excitement – a kind of primitive blood-lust – seemed to grip the shooting party. Each member appeared to be trying to outshoot his neighbour and the birds began to fall out of the air like leaves.

Makepeace, Dempsey noted, was blasting away just as enthusiastically as any of them. It was another side of her he hadn't seen before, he reflected soberly. Here, on her home ground, she seemed a different person entirely. The usual gulf between them had become even wider.

He ran his eye along the line, lingering for a time on Frances Trafford's imposing figure, then moving on to the others. In the distance, he saw with surprise, was the Chinese official, Ch'ien, looking incongruous in a Mao jacket with a deerstalker hat on his head. But judging by the way he was hitting his feathery targets he had obviously had plenty of previous experience at shoots such as this. Another odd piece of information to be filed away for future reference, Dempsey decided.

Eventually tiring of watching the slaughter, Dempsey headed away to do some exploring on his own. Moving parallel to the shooting line he wandered towards a small wood he'd noticed earlier.

It was cool and quiet within the trees, the gunfire suddenly seeming much farther away. Feeling safe from any prying eyes he decided to risk removing his jacket and revealing the .44 Magnum.

He spent several minutes wandering through the copse, soaking up the atmosphere and watching intently for any sign of the wildlife he could hear rustling around him. Finally he caught sight of a fat rabbit that broke cover ahead of him and scampered between the trees, before disappearing under a bush.

Dempsey continued on as silently as he could, hoping to encounter other animals.

Then he heard it – the faintest of clicks behind him. Instinctively he flung himself flat on the ground. And as the side of his face hit the carpet of leaves there was a deafening explosion, and the trunk of a nearby tree suddenly lost a large section of its bark as a cloud of shotgun pellets tore into it.

Dempsey reacted with ruthless speed. The .44 was in his hand without seeming to move from the holster. He twisted his body round and fired three shots in swift succession at the bushes behind him.

He waited as the echoes of the shots died away. Then he sprang to his feet and took cover behind the tree. He stayed crouching there, the Magnum trained on the bushes, for some thirty seconds. There were no more shots. In fact, no sounds at all.

Warily he emerged from behind the tree and moved towards the bushes. There was no one there, nor was there any sign of blood. He had apparently missed with all three bullets.

He continued on through the copse, ears straining for the slightest of noises.

And then he found him. He was lying on his back, the shot gun by his side.

Dempsey's stomach did a slow forward-roll as he stared at him. 'Jesus . . .' he muttered.

There was a rustling in the bushes. He spun round, the Magnum ready to fire.

Makepeace burst out of the bushes. She started to say something and then noticed the figure on the ground. Her eyes went wide with horror. 'What happened?' she finally gasped.

'I think I've killed your father,' said Dempsey.

CHAPTER SIXTEEN

Lord Winfield lay in his magnificent Jacobean four-poster bed. His face was deathly pale apart from the long purple bruise that stretched from above his right cheek to his chin.

There were four other people in the bedroom: Makepeace, Dempsey, Naismith and a short, portly gentleman called Potter. The latter was Lord Winfield's doctor and he was shaking his head with disapproval as his patient refused yet again to be taken to hospital.

'Really Roy, I'm fine,' said Lord Winfield weakly. 'Just had the wind knocked out of my sails, that's all.'

'I still think you should have an X-ray,' said Potter. 'A blow like that is no laughing matter for a man your age, Freddie.'

'And I say I'm not going to any damn hospital and that's final. Thanks for rushing over here and for everything you've done but I think you might as well leave now.'

Potter sighed and picked his medical bag up from the bedside table. 'You're an obstinate old fool, Freddie.' He turned to Makepeace. 'Call me if there's any problem. I'll look in later tonight. In the meantime make sure he stays in bed.'

'I will,' she promised him. 'Naismith, please see the doctor out.'

When Naismith and Dr Potter had left the room Makepeace took hold of her father's hand and gazed down at him worriedly. 'I wish you'd done as he wanted, Daddy.'

'Not you too, Harriet. It was just a bang on the jaw. I've had a lot worse in my time.'

'But you were unconscious for nearly an hour. You might have brain damage.'

'Oh, tommy-rot!' snorted Lord Winfield. 'But I'd certainly like to inflict some brain damage on whoever it was who hit me . . .'

Dempsey, who'd been standing in the background, came forward. 'You still can't remember the guy's face?' he asked.

'No,' sighed Lord Winfield. 'It all happened so quickly. All I saw was a blur. I heard a shotgun go off nearby, then I heard what sounded like a heavy calibre handgun – which I now know was yours – and then someone came running towards me through the bushes. I was just turning to see who it was when wham! the butt of this shotgun hit me in the face.'

'And you're sure you didn't see anyone entering the woods before you did?' asked Dempsey.

'Not a soul. All I saw was the fat pheasant I'd been stalking.'

Dempsey rubbed his chin. 'Maybe someone mistook me for a fat pheasant . . . but I doubt it. When they saw they'd missed me they ran off – and ran straight into you. They knocked you out to prevent you from identifying them.'

'But who would want to kill you, James?' asked Lord Winfield. 'And why?'

'Someone obviously knows the real reason I'm here. Have you told anyone I'm a cop?'

'Not a soul.'

'Then they put two and two together somehow. And it worries them. Which suggests the jade is still on the premises.'

Makepeace said, 'I think it's time you got some rest, Daddy.' She squeezed his hand. 'We'll talk again later.'

He sighed and nodded. 'Yes, darling. I believe I could do with a little sleep.'

'Come on, Dempsey,' said Makepeace and led the way out of the room.

In the corridor outside she took a deep breath and leaned her head back with her eyes closed. She seemed to sway a little.

'You OK?' Dempsey asked, concerned.

She let the breath out in a long, shuddering sigh then nodded. 'Yes. I'm still a bit shaky, that's all. I haven't recovered yet from seeing Daddy lying there in the woods.' She looked at Dempsey. 'I thought you had shot him.'

'So did I for a while. It was one of the worst moments of my life.'

'I almost shot you, you know,' she told him grimly. 'I came very close to letting go with both barrels.'

He shrugged. 'That's understandable. But you didn't, so let's drop it.'

She reached over and, briefly, put her hand on his arm without saying anything.

Feeling embarrassed, Dempsey said quickly, 'What I was saying in there, about someone knowing I'm a cop and trying to kill me. It applies to you too. You're in danger as well.'

'So what do we do?'

'We act very carefully and we wait. Someone will crawl out of the woodwork for another attempt. Let's hope we get them before they get us.'

They then went down to the main hall. All the guests were gathered there, anxious to hear how Lord Winfield was. As Makepeace circulated among them, reassuring everybody as to her father's condition, Dempsey stayed on the side lines, keeping a surreptitious eye on them all.

Some minutes later he was rewarded with the sight of Frances Trafford having a brief but intense whispered exchange with Naismith. The expression he glimpsed on her face told Dempsey that this was no ordinary conversation between an employee of Lord Winfield's and one of his guests.

Dinner that night was a subdued affair and afterwards most of the guests retired early. Two exceptions were Selwyn King and Andrew Sims who played billiards until past midnight. Dempsey kept them company in the billiard room, carefully nursing a single brandy while they steadily became inebriated. He had the strong suspicion he would need to stay sober this night.

When they finally went to bed Dempsey went in search of Makepeace. He found her coming along the corridor from her father's room.

'How is he?' he asked her.

'Sleeping peacefully. Dr Potter had another look at him tonight and said he still didn't seem to be showing any symptoms of concussion, or worse, though he'd still prefer him to be in hospital.'

Dempsey told her of the odd exchange he'd witnessed between Naismith and Frances Trafford.

'You think that's who she was referring to last night in your room?' she asked, frowning. 'But why on earth would Frances be scared of Naismith? Disgusted by him, yes, but scared? It doesn't make any sense.'

'Well, I think I may just mosey along to her room right now and discuss the situation with her.'

Makepeace raised an eyebrow. 'Want me to come with you?'

'No. Be better if I speak to her alone.'

'Better for whom?'

Dempsey contrived to look surprised. 'Hey, what do you think I am? This is pure business. I just think she's more likely to open up if I'm alone.'

'No comment,' said Makepeace dryly.

'In the meantime you go and change into something dark. Black, if possible. I want you to spend the night keeping an eye out for anything suspicious. My guess is that whoever stole the jade is getting nervous. They may try to recover it from its hiding place and make a run for it.'

She nodded. 'I know every sound in this house.

115

Every creak in every floorboard. Anyone moves, I'll know.'

'Good. But don't take any chances. You armed?'

She nodded.

'Okay. I'll meet you down in the main hall in, say, thirty minutes.'

'You think it will only take that long to have Frances revealing her innermost secrets to you?'

'If last night's performance is any indication it won't even take that long.' He grinned at her and turned to go, then he hesitated. 'Oh, Makepeace, when your radar-like ears tell you someone is coming your way, make sure it's not me before you swing into action.'

'Funny. I was about to make the same request of you.'

A light still showed under Frances Trafford's door. Dempsey knocked gently. There was a long pause before he heard a nervous voice say, 'Who is it? Who's there?'

'It's me, Dempsey.'

The door was unlocked and opened a few inches. She peered out at him. 'What do you want?' she asked suspiciously.

Dempsey began to think it was going to take longer than thirty minutes after all. 'I want to talk to you. Can I come in?'

She hesitated, then opened the door the rest of the way. As he stepped into the room she shut it quickly.

She was wearing the same black nightdress she'd had on the night before but that was the only thing the same about her, apart from the smell of alcohol on her breath. She looked older somehow; crumpled. There was no hint of the previous night's sensuality and sexual hunger.

She stared at him with nervous, haunted eyes. 'About last night . . .' she began.

116

He held up a hand. 'Hey, no sweat. I understand. You had a few too many under your belt. No need to feel bad about it.'

'I acted very foolishly. There's no two ways about it.'

She went and sat on the edge of her bed. Dempsey noticed a half full bottle of vodka and three bottles of pills on the bedside table. He walked over and picked up one of the pill containers. The label had 'Phenobarbitone' on it. He picked up a second bottle. Its label read 'Thenotrate'. The third bottle contained amphetamine tablets.

'Pills to put you to sleep and pills to get you up. And vodka. A lethal combination,' he said.

'I have trouble sleeping. A lot of trouble.'

'Any particular reason?'

'None that you'd be interested in.'

'Is Naismith one of them?'

She gave a start of surprise. 'How . . .?'

'It's my job to know these things. I'm a cop.'

She nodded slowly. 'Yes. He said you were.'

It was Dempsey's turn to be surprised. 'How did he find out?'

Dryly, she said, 'It's his job to know these things. He's a slimy, crooked, little blackmailer.'

Dempsey gave a grim smile. 'And he's blackmailing you?'

'Yes.' She picked up the bottle of vodka and took several swallows.

'Want to tell me about it?'

'No, but I will. I've got to tell someone. I can't go on like this any longer.' Her eyes filled with tears. 'It's all because of my husband, Richard. He was a famous archaeologist, you know . . . there was talk of a knighthood . . .' Her voice faltered, then she went on, 'I loved him, but the marriage wasn't really a success. To be blunt, we weren't sexually compatible. So eventually I started having affairs. I was discreet but Richard

117

found out. It shattered him . . .' She closed her eyes. The tears were now running down her cheeks.

'What did he do?' asked Dempsey.

'He killed himself.'

'Oh . . .'

'The official story was that he died of typhoid in the north of Thailand but in reality he drowned himself in a river. There was a cover-up between the Thai government and the Foreign Office to avoid embarrassment on both sides. And Richard's family is very influential . . . and very rich. It's because of them I'm in this mess.'

'I don't follow.'

'His family know he committed suicide but they don't know why he did. If they did find out the reason I'd never get another penny from them. You see, Richard never had much money of his own – he would have inherited part of a fortune when his father died, of course, but in the meantime the family supported him, and me. Very generously too. And that support has continued since Richard's death.'

Dempsey nodded. 'I see.' He was beginning to get the picture now. 'And Naismith knows the truth. How did he find out?'

'I was staying here at the time. Freddie kindly invited me here to recover from the shock of Richard's death. I was here a couple of months and during that period Richard's personal effects arrived from Thailand. I had them sent here. There weren't many – just a small suitcase with some clothes, notebooks and diaries. But hidden in one of the diaries I found an envelope addressed to me. It was a letter from Richard. He wrote it the day he killed himself. He told me he knew all about my various lovers . . . he told me how much pain I'd caused him . . . that I'd destroyed him by my unfaithfulness and that he was going to . . . to commit suicide . . .'

She took another drink from the vodka bottle. 'I

118

should have destroyed it, but I didn't. And Naismith found it. He goes through everyone's things here all the time. He's a habitual snoop.'

'And he threatened to show the letter to your husband's family?'

She nodded. 'And he's been blackmailing me ever since.'

'What form do the payments take?'

'Money and . . . other things.'

'Sex, you mean?'

'Yes.' Her shoulders sagged. Her face had grown more haggard. She looked at him with defeated eyes. 'You wouldn't believe some of the things he's made me do. He enjoys humiliating me, making me suffer . . .'

A tight ball of anger was growing inside Dempsey. He was looking forward to getting his hands on Naismith.

'There's more,' she said reluctantly. 'He's made me his accomplice in another blackmail scheme. I'm in so deep now I'll never get out . . .'

'Tell me.'

'A couple of months ago when I was here one of Freddie's old friends came down for the weekend. He's a cabinet minister. Naismith made me proposition him. We made love . . . and Naismith took pictures with a concealed camera. Now he's making me blackmail the politician on his behalf.'

'Shit,' muttered Dempsey.

'You see what I mean? I'll never get out of this mess. I can't resist Naismith. I have no will-power anymore. He can make me do whatever he wants, and the things he asks are becoming more and more terrible . . .'

She took a deep breath and shuddered. 'This morning he ordered me to kill you.'

CHAPTER SEVENTEEN

'So it was you who shot at me this morning in the woods!' said Dempsey, surprised.

She shook her head. 'No, no . . . I couldn't go through with it. No matter what threats Naismith makes I can't commit murder . . .'

He regarded her carefully for a time and then decided she was telling the truth. That meant it had been someone else who'd tried to kill him. But who? Naismith himself, forced to do his own dirty work? It seemed the most likely answer.

'I think it's time I had a little talk with your friend Naismith,' he said quietly.

She jumped up, her face showing alarm. 'Oh no, don't! Not yet! Not tonight! Give me some time . . . I'm not ready.' She clung to him, burying her face against his shoulder. Her body shook as she began to sob.

Gently as he could he disengaged himself from her embrace. 'It's got to be done now. You'll be fine. Don't worry. Try to get some sleep . . .'

'Please don't leave me alone,' she pleaded. 'Stay with me tonight. I'm frightened. I need to be with someone . . .'

'I'm sorry but I can't. Take one of your pills and go to bed. I'll talk to you in the morning.'

Her tear-streaked face became accusing. 'Is that all you can say? Is that the best you can do? You're a great help, Dempsey. A great help . . .' She turned her back on him.

Dempsey couldn't think of anything else to say to her. Feeling acutely uncomfortable he quietly opened the door and withdrew.

He went to the Great Hall and peered into its

shadowy interior, trying to see if Makepeace was there yet.

'Makepeace?' he whispered into the darkness. There was no sign of her.

'I'm here.' Her voice came from directly behind him. He turned, surprised. Makepeace stepped out from the shadow of an alcove. She had followed his instructions to dress in dark clothing to the letter. She was wearing a black track suit, sneakers and had concealed her blonde hair under a black scarf. All that was missing was shoe polish on her face.

'Very impressive,' he admitted.

'So what happened with the Widow Trafford? Did she melt under the intense beam of your charm and tell you everything?'

'She talked okay, but because she's scared shitless. Our pal Naismith has got her by the pubic hairs, literally. He's blackmailing her.'

Makepeace gave a shocked gasp. 'Good Lord. I can't believe it! What on earth could he blackmail Frances about?'

'I can't tell you, yet, but it's bad, real bad . . .'

She was silent for a few seconds then said, 'You think then he's the one behind everything? The missing jade, the attempt on your life . . . Daddy being hit?'

'Let's just say that on a suspect-rating scale of one to ten he gets a nine and a half in my book. I think we should go interrupt his beauty sleep. Show me the way to his room . . .'

Makepeace led the way to the servants' quarters in the rear of the house. They moved as quietly as possible along the corridor, Makepeace using a pencil flashlight that she'd picked up in her room while changing. Finally she stopped outside one of the bedroom doors. 'This is it,' she said.

Dempsey tried the door handle. It wasn't locked. He opened the door a few inches. 'Let's surprise him,' he whispered to Makepeace.

Silently, they entered Naismith's bedroom. Make-peace aimed the narrow torch beam at the bed. It was empty. She swung the beam right around the room. Naismith wasn't there.

'Shit,' muttered Dempsey.

'Now what?'

'We wait.'

They took position on each side of the door. Minutes passed. After they'd been waiting in silence for a quarter of an hour Makepeace said softly, 'What if he's decided to make a run for it? If he is the one who stole the jade maybe he's gone to wherever he hid it and plans to make his getaway with it tonight . . .'

'Yeah,' said Dempsey sourly. 'I been thinking the same thing. Let's split up. You search the house, I'll take the grounds.'

'Why don't we both search outside? You know the jade is more likely to be hidden somewhere on the estate rather than in the house.'

'Do as I say. I don't want the two of us to be running around out there in the dark.'

'You can't give me orders, Dempsey. And I know exactly what you're thinking – that it's more dangerous outside.'

'We're wasting time. Stop arguing and get moving.'

'I'm coming with you.'

Dempsey sighed and tried a different tack. 'One of us should stay inside and as you know every inch of the house so well it should be you. Or do you want to leave your father unguarded?'

'What do you mean?'

'Look, there's a would-be killer on the loose around here, so don't you think you should stay within easy reach of your father until we get the guy?'

'You're a sod, Dempsey.'

'I know. So you'll do as I say?'

'Yes.'

'Good. Fire a shot if you need me back in a hurry. I'll

do the same outside. Otherwise let's rendezvous back in the main hall in an hour.'

'Right. Here, you'd better take this.' She handed him the flashlight. 'You'll need it more than I will.'

Dempsey went out through the door that led into the rose garden, where the drinks had been served earlier in the evening. He stood there for a while, letting his eyes adjust to the darkness. It was a clear night and the three-quarter full moon provided some illumination though not much.

Then he began to move, listening intently for any sound. After satisfying himself that there was no one in the rose garden, he left it and started to cross the wide expanse of lawn that stretched down to the shore of the ornamental lake.

As he crept through the darkness he felt his senses become increasingly attuned to the night. Old instincts that he hadn't used since his days in Vietnam were reviving again, and with them came an adrenalin-charged feeling of excitement.

He reached the shore of the lake and stared at its black, calm surface. Nearby he could just distinguish the outline of the small stone and wood jetty.

As he stood there a sudden thought struck him. *Of course!* he told himself. The perfect hiding place for the jade. Underwater! He cursed himself for not thinking of it before.

Quickly he went over to the jetty and walked out to the end of it. He peered down at the water. Where would *he* have hidden the jade in the lake? Some place where it would be easy to recover in a hurry. Maybe right near the jetty itself, or under it . . .

He came to a decision. He stripped off down to his shorts then, with the pencil flashlight gripped between his teeth, lowered himself off the end of the jetty.

The water was not only freezing, it was also deeper than he expected. It had reached his neck before his feet touched the bottom. He shuddered with distaste. The lake bottom felt unpleasantly slimy.

Got to get this over with as quickly as possible, he thought. This is not fun.

He switched the flashlight on and peered under the jetty, hoping to see a tell-tale line tied there; a line that would hopefully have a weighted, plastic bag full of jade on the other end of it.

He couldn't see anything, so he started to move round to one side of the jetty . . . As he moved he felt his bare right foot hit something. Something soft . . .

He froze as bubbles broke the surface and what felt like human fingers brush against his thigh.

Then, with nightmare slowness, a head rose up out of the water only inches away from his own.

He found himself face to face with Frances Trafford. And she was dead. Very dead.

CHAPTER EIGHTEEN

Makepeace gave a startled gasp as the hand touched her on the shoulder. She spun round, reaching for the .38 revolver tucked against the small of her back.

'Hey, easy,' whispered a familiar voice. 'It's only me.' A light suddenly appeared, illuminating Dempsey's face.

Angrily she said, 'What's the idea of sneaking up on me like that? I nearly shot you. And anyway I thought we were supposed to rendezvous down in the Great Hall.'

Dempsey switched off the flashlight. 'Sorry, but I had to find you in a hurry. We got a problem.'

'Another one? What is it?'

'Frances Trafford. I found her skinny dipping in the lake. Trouble is she's dead.'

'Oh no . . .'

'Could be suicide but my bet is murder. Either way I feel pretty disgusted with myself. She begged me not to leave her alone.'

'But you had no way of knowing . . .'

'I should have known. She was trying to tell me something, but I wasn't listening.' He took a deep breath. 'Let's check out Naismith's room again. This time I got a hunch we'll find him there. And boy, is he gonna do some talking!'

When they arrived at Naismith's room they saw his light was on. They could also hear the murmur of angry voices from inside. Naismith was obviously arguing with someone. Dempsey drew his gun and motioned Makepeace to do the same. Then he knocked on the door.

The voices stopped. Dempsey knocked again. Then someone in the room yelled, 'No!'

Dempsey reached for the door handle and was just beginning to turn it when the door suddenly shuddered; and the pointed steel head of a spear came crashing through the wood only a few inches from Dempsey's right ear.

'Jesus,' he muttered and ducked to one side.

'How charming,' said Makepeace. 'I get the feeling they want to be left alone.'

Dempsey shone the flashlight on the spear. It protruded some nine inches out of the splintered wood. 'Look.'

'Ugh.'

Blood was trickling down the door.

'I don't think that was meant for me after all,' said Dempsey. He reached for the door handle again and turned it. Then he thrust the door open and sprang into the room, the Magnum cocked and ready to fire.

Makepeace followed him. But they saw at a glance that the room was empty. Apart from Naismith.

He was pinned to the door, the spear sticking through his throat. The front of his suit and the floor were covered in blood.

'The killer must have got out through there,' said Makepeace, indicating the open French windows. 'It's the only other exit.'

Dempsey went and looked out. The windows opened onto a small balcony. Nearby was a stout drainpipe. There were also plenty of hand-holds in the wall. It would be an easy climb down to the ground. He scanned the bushes for any sign of movement but could see nothing.

He returned to Naismith. The dead secretary's eyes bulged with an expression of shocked amazement. 'How could this have happened to *me*?' was their silent message. Dempsey reached up and closed them. Then he pointed at the dead man's feet. 'Look. His shoes are at least five inches from the floor. We're dealing with one strong son-of-a-bitch here. The guy had enough strength to pick Naismith up with one hand and drive a spear right through him and a thick door with the other.'

'Which lets out Biffin or Selwyn,' said Makepeace.

'But not Sims . . . or Ch'ien.' Dempsey went over to a large writing desk. Its drawers were open and there were papers scattered about. 'Looks like someone was looking for something. Without success. Why don't you try and find what it is? Go over the room inch by inch. Use your imagination.'

'I'll remember to look under the mattress,' she said wryly.

He wasn't amused. 'And look in the mattress too. Rip it to shreds if necessary.'

'And what will you be doing?'

'I'm going to discuss East-West relations with the inscrutable Mr Ch'ien. Then I'll pay a social call on the Sims.'

Gun in hand, Dempsey tapped lightly on Ch'ien's bedroom door. He waited but there was no response. Quietly, he opened the door and stepped into the darkened room. The only light came from the large window. Its curtains were pushed back and it was open.

When his eyes had adjusted to the gloom he looked carefully around the room. The bed was empty and, like the rest of the room, in pristine condition. There was only one hint of human habitation – a sweet, spicy smell in the air.

Dempsey found its source. A single joss-stick burning in a small vase on the bedside table.

He went to the bathroom door and opened it. There was no one there. He gave it a quick inspection but like the bedroom it was pristine.

More scrabbling. Then a hand appeared over the top of the balcony. Makepeace's finger tensed on the finger.

A head rose into view.

Makepeace let out her breath in a long sigh.

'Don't just stand there. Give me some help,' growled Dempsey.

Makepeace lowered the gun. 'That's the second time tonight I've almost shot you,' she told him angrily.

'Third time lucky,' he panted, as he hauled himself over the balcony railing and then removed the heavy knapsack and dumped it on the floor. 'I was sure I saw someone out there heading in this direction. I followed him but lost him in the bushes down below. I take it you haven't had any visitors?'

'Nary a soul.' She looked at the knapsack. 'What's in there?'

He opened it and showed her. She gave a low whistle.

'I found it in Ch'ien's room. My guess that the jade is in the lake must be right.'

'So Ch'ien is the one.'

'Looks like it.'

'But why would he steal it if Daddy is going to be made to hand it over to the Chinese government anyway?'

'Maybe Ch'ien is a ringer. Maybe he doesn't work for the Chinese government at all.'

Makepeace looked closer at the diving gear. 'It's wet,' she said.

'Yeah. Used recently. Very recently.'

'But for what? Was Ch'ien recovering the jade or . . .?'

'Or murdering Frances Trafford.'

Makepeace frowned and glanced at Naismith. 'So where does he figure in all of this?'

'The only explanation is that he and Ch'ien were working together. Maybe Ch'ien was working for Naismith.'

129

'But then they had a disagreement. A serious one.'

'Have you found anything yet?'

She shook her head. 'No. And I've looked everywhere. Even in his pockets.'

Dempsey looked at the writing desk. 'What about that thing? That's where they were looking before we arrived.'

'That "thing" is an escritoire. And yes, I have searched it thoroughly.'

Dempsey went and examined it, running his fingers over its top. 'Any secret drawers in this escritoire?'

'There is one, yes.' She walked across, reached under a shelf and touched a hidden lever. A small, spring-loaded drawer popped out from the front of the desk. It was empty.

'Any more?' he asked.

'No.'

'You sound certain.'

'I should be. This piece of furniture has been in my family for generations.'

He grinned at her. 'Since the Restoration?'

'Anyone with half an eye should recognize this as a Victorian mahogany cylinder escritoire,' she told him stiffly.

Dempsey felt under the secret drawer. There was a sound of adhesive tape being peeled off. He then slapped a slim manilla envelope onto the desk top. 'And a policewoman with half a brain should recognize this as a piece of vital evidence.'

Makepeace blushed. 'Bugger.'

She watched as Dempsey opened it carefully and extracted several papers. He examined them and frowned. 'Copies of Interpol crime sheets. List of offences long as your arm. Has this guy been active.'

'Who?'

'Someone called Hoffman. Harold Hoffman.'

'Doesn't ring any bells.'

'Maybe it was an alias of Naismith's.'

130

'Possibly. Sure can't be Ch'ien, unless he's wearing a hell of a clever disguise.' Dempsey folded the paper and put them in his pocket. 'Whoever Hoffman is he's suspected of carrying out nearly a dozen murders in various countries. The guy's a pro . . .'

'So now what?'

'I think I'll go see if our Chinese friend is back from his nocturnal wanderings.'

'What about me?'

'Stay here and keep an eye on that diving gear. I'm gonna need it later. You can keep Naismith company at the same time. He looks kinda depressed.'

CHAPTER NINETEEN

Ch'ien was sitting up in bed, a hardback book resting on his lap. Apart from the sheet covering the lower half of his body he appeared to be naked. Dempsey saw that his torso was heavily muscled to a remarkable degree and his biceps looked like melons. There was more than enough strength in those arms to have picked up Naismith and stapled him to his bedroom door.

'Mr Dempsey!' said Ch'ien with surprise as Dempsey entered. 'What is the matter? Why are you up at this hour?'

'We think there's a prowler in the house. I'm checking all the bedrooms,' lied Dempsey easily.

'A prowler? Do you need my assistance?'

'No. Naismith and I can handle it okay.'

Dempsey watched to see if Ch'ien reacted to the mention of Naismith but his eyes betrayed nothing. 'You haven't seen or heard anyone, have you?'

Ch'ien shook his head.

'Mr Ch'ien, this is the second time I've been here. I came several minutes ago but you weren't here. Where were you?'

Ch'ien lifted the book from his lap. 'I was down in the library, looking for something to read. I'm an insomniac.'

Dempsey read the title of the book. 'Dr No?'

Ch'ien gave an apologetic smile. 'I confess a weakness for Western thrillers, Mr Dempsey. The more far-fetched the better.'

'Sure,' said Dempsey, sounding unconvinced. He glanced round the room. 'What's that?' he asked, pointing at the pool of water in front of the wardrobe.

Ch'ien frowned. 'I'm sure I have no idea.'

Dempsey went over to the wardrobe and opened it. He looked at Ch'ien. Again his eyes betrayed nothing. If he was surprised at seeing the knapsack gone he was doing a good job of concealing it.

'Were you storing something wet in there?' Dempsey asked him.

'No. I can't imagine where that water could have come from.'

Dempsey shut the door. 'Well, Mr Ch'ien, if you do happen to hear or see anyone I'd sure appreciate it if you'd come and tell either me or Mr Naismith, okay?'

'Of course I will, Mr Dempsey.'

Dempsey started to leave but paused at the door and turned round. 'Mr Ch'ien, you Chinese read right from left, yeah?'

Ch'ien smiled at him. 'That is correct, Mr Dempsey. Chinese characters are read right to left.'

'But you don't read upside-down?'

Ch'ien's smile broadened. 'No, Mr Dempsey. We don't read upside-down.'

'Then why, Mr Ch'ien, are you holding the book upside-down?'

Ch'ien glanced at the book on his lap and the smile abruptly disappeared from his face.

'Goodnight, Mr Ch'ien,' said Dempsey with a grin, and left.

'Well?' asked Makepeace.

'Inscrutable as ever but I did penetrate a chink in his armour, as you would say.' Dempsey described their encounter to her.

'But he wasn't in the least surprised to see that his diving equipment was gone?' she asked.

'Nope. He's either a hell of a good actor or . . .'

'Or what?'

'He didn't even know it had been there.'

133

'You mean someone planted it in his room?'

'It's a possibility. The mysterious Mr Hoffman, maybe. But even if the gear isn't Ch'ien's, he was definitely up to something fishy tonight. I don't buy his insomnia crap.'

Dempsey knelt down beside the knapsack and pulled out the air bottles. The pressure gauge showed there was just over fifteen minutes of air left.

He frowned. 'Not much, but it's maybe enough.'

'Enough for what?'

'For me to find the jade in the lake. I'm going for another swim.'

'Okay. I'll come and watch.'

'No.' He reached into his pocket and produced the Interpol crime sheets. 'Call Spikings and tell him we need information on this name, urgently.'

'Call the Chief at this time of the night?'

'No, Makepeace. Call him at this time of the morning. And tell him what's been happening here as well, but that we don't want the local cops moving in to take the bodies away until we've flushed out the killer. Got it?'

She nodded. 'But if you don't mind I'll make the call from my own room. I'm beginning to find Naismith's company rather boring.'

Carrying the knapsack on his back Dempsey hurried across the lawns down towards the jetty. He scanned the surroundings for any sign of movement but there was none. Or at least none that he could see.

Before going onto the jetty he checked the bushes where he had hidden Frances Trafford's body. She was still there; a long, white object in the shadows. A couple of hours ago that body had been warm and alive – a human being – now it was nothing but an inconvenience. Something to be got rid of, like a discarded junk food box.

He went out to the end of the jetty and quickly stripped off again. He wasn't looking forward to what he was about to do. The nearest thing he had to a weakness was a fear of enclosed spaces. It wasn't anything like a fully fledged case of claustrophobia but it was enough to bother him occasionally. And he knew that scuba diving, especially at night, was guaranteed to bring it on.

He was confident he could handle the fear but offhand he could think of a million things he'd rather be doing than going down into that black water.

He strapped on the air bottles, which were designed to hang against the chest instead of on your back, then put the mouthpiece into position and checked the air flow. Satisfied the unit was working, he put on the flippers and, after washing it out, the face mask.

Then, with the strap of the underwater flashlight wrapped firmly around his wrist, he lowered himself into the water.

He expelled the air from his lungs and let himself sink under the surface. Even with the wetsuit jacket on it was brutally cold and he wondered if he would be able to stand it for even the whole fifteen minutes he had of air supply.

He kicked away from the jetty and switched on the light. The beam had difficulty in penetrating the murky water and he realized that finding anything in this pea soup was going to be hard.

He gazed down at the bottom of the lake which was covered with weeds and then began a slow search back and forth in front of the jetty, going further out with each pass.

The general eeriness of this bleak, silent world soon started playing tricks with his imagination. He began seeing things out of the corner of his eye; things that vanished when he turned to look at them. At one point he thought he glimpsed the long, white body of Frances Trafford swimming beside him through the gloom . . .

Cut the crap, Dempsey! he told himself angrily. He knew that panic had killed more divers than anything else underwater, so he forced his mind clear of all its

135

fears and phantoms and concentrated on the job of looking for the jade.

He had only a couple of minutes of air left when he spotted the plastic bag lying amongst the weeds. It had a heavy chain attached to it. He swam quickly to it. Through the thick, clear plastic he saw something green illuminated by the torch beam.

He removed the chain and carried the bag up to the surface. He felt a tremendous sense of relief as his head broke the surface and realized his nerves had been stretched near to breaking point down there on the bottom. As far as he was concerned that was the last night dive he was going to make for a long, long time.

He switched off the air and looked around to get his bearings. It was hard to see anything at first but then he spotted the outline of the jetty. It was about twenty yards away.

Trailing the bag behind him he struck out for it. When he reached it he heaved the jade out of the water and, with difficulty, placed it on the jetty. Then he started to haul himself up onto the jetty.

He was just about to swing his right leg up when he saw a blur of motion coming straight at him along the jetty.

He had no time to react. He saw the bare foot and felt it explode under his chin almost simultaneously. His head snapped back and, with a grunt, he was sent flying backwards into the water.

He felt himself slowly sinking down into the blackness; a blackness far, far deeper than any lake.

CHAPTER TWENTY

The phone rang. Makepeace snatched it up before the second ring had even begun. 'That you, Chief?'

'What other poor sod would be calling you at ten to three in the bloody morning, Makepeace?' came the unmistakable voice of Spikings down the line.

Makepeace smiled. He sounded much less annoyed than when she'd spoken to him half an hour ago. His language then had been so colourful and inventive, she'd thought she'd have to run a tap over the receiver to cool it down. 'What's the word on Hoffman?'

'According to the computer it's an alias belonging to a professional crook wanted in several European countries as well as the States. Usually operates with his sister. No one knows their real names but the aliases they use a lot of the time are Nicholas and Joyce Agee. Ring any bells?'

She felt disappointed. 'No. None . . . What are they wanted for?'

'Murder, mostly. When they're not committing robberies they hire themselves out as freelance killers. I've got a list of their other aliases. I'll read them out.'

Makepeace listened as Spikings went down the list of names. Suddenly she cried, 'The last two, Chief!'

'Andrew and Susan Sims?'

'Yes. They're here. Staying at the house.'

There was a pause at the other end of the line. Then, uncharacteristically, Spikings said softly, 'Better play it carefully, Harry. These two are right bastards. You want me to send the troops in?'

'No, not yet. Dempsey wants more time. He wants to recover the jade first to flush them out into the open.'

'Well, warn Dempsey about who you're up against as soon as you can.'

'I will, Chief, in fact I think I hear him coming now. I'll keep you posted. Bye.' She hung up and turned. The door opened.

Dempsey was drowning. The water was pouring into his nose and mouth, choking him as he struggled back to consciousness.

It was the cold that saved him, shocking him swiftly back to full awareness. He remembered where he was, what has happening . . .

His instinct was to get his head above the surface immediately but he fought against it. His attacker would be waiting and watching.

So he stayed underwater, groping his way towards the jetty. His hands touched one of the supports; he kept going until he was certain he was under the jetty. Only then did he stand up.

Dempsey sucked in the air gratefully, trying not to cough. He couldn't afford to make a sound. Above him he heard the wood creak as his attacker moved along the jetty.

Dempsey put the end of the air hose back into his mouth. He knew the tanks were almost empty but he was confident there was enough air left for what he was going to do.

He submerged again and made his way out from under the side of the jetty. Then, very cautiously, he raised his head until just the top of the face mask was exposed.

At the end of the jetty, clearly outlined in the moonlight, was Ch'ien. He was leaning forward, peering at the spot where Dempsey had vanished. He was naked apart from a loincloth.

Dempsey didn't hesitate. He crept along the side of the jetty until he reached the end corner. Then he grabbed Ch'ien's right ankle and pulled with all his strength.

The Chinaman hit the water with a loud splash. Dempsey was on him before he could orientate himself. He got Ch'ien in a stranglehold and, using all his weight, bore down on him, pushing his head under the water.

Although he was at a disadvantage, Ch'ien fought back with lethal ferocity, his fingers gouging into Dempsey's flesh like claws of steel. Dempsey tried to ignore the pain and put all his effort into keeping Ch'ien underwater.

Ch'ien changed his tactics. He began pummelling Dempsey in the stomach with one of his fists. His strength was awesome. Dempsey felt he was being hit with a sledgehammer. The pain exploded through him and he found he couldn't draw breath, but he continued to hang on to Ch'ien, keeping him down.

Finally Ch'ien's struggles grew weaker and then ceased altogether. His body went limp but Dempsey didn't relax the grip on his neck. He counted slowly. When he got to thirty he let go of the Chinaman and stood up.

For a time all he could do was suck air in greedily, then he turned his attention to Ch'ien. His body had floated to the surface and he was lying there face-down.

Dempsey turned him over and then began to tow him to the shore. He was exhausted by the time he'd hauled the heavy body up the grassy bank and collapsed onto his hands and knees. He ached all over and felt nauseous from the amount of lake water he'd swallowed. Most painful of all was his lower jaw where Ch'ien had kicked him.

Wearily he climbed out of the harness and dropped the air tanks on the grass, then he bent over Ch'ien to see if he was breathing.

He was taken completely by surprise when the

Chinaman's fist flashed upwards and slammed into the side of his head.

Dempsey, stunned, was sent rolling down the bank. Ch'ien sprang to his feet and came after him. As Dempsey managed to brake himself on the grassy slope Ch'ien kicked him hard in the ribs. Dempsey almost blacked out from the pain but instinctively lashed out with his hand. His fingers closed around Ch'ien's ankle as the Chinaman's foot thudded into his chest for the second time. Dempsey clung onto the ankle, then grabbed the foot with his other hand as well. He gave it a sharp wrench.

Ch'ien grunted fell. Dempsey jumped up, remembering an old ju-jitsu hold from his army combat training days. Still keeping his grip on Ch'ien's right foot he lifted it upwards, at the same time planting his own foot hard on the inner side of Ch'ien's left foot. Then he began twisting the right foot outwards.

Ch'ien screamed. He was helpless and the pain, Dempsey knew, must have been excruciating. He squirmed and writhed impotently, arching his back and flailing his arms. Dempsey kept twisting. Ch'ien's scream turned into a ragged sob.

'Give up,' panted Dempsey, 'or I'll dislocate every joint in your goddamn leg.'

'Yes . . . yes . . .' hissed Ch'ien. 'I'll do anything you say, only stop . . .'

Dempsey started to relax his grip. It was a mistake. Ch'ien wrenched his foot out of his hands and then kicked him in the throat. Dempsey reeled backwards, trying to breathe. He was only vaguely aware of being grabbed by Ch'ien, lifted into the air and flung a considerable distance.

He landed heavily on something hard. He realized it was the breathing unit. He rolled to one side and grabbed hold of the straps of the harness. Then he lurched to his feet.

Ch'ien was coming at him in a deadly rush, his

muscular body crouched low, his massive arms spread wide to envelop Dempsey in a crushing embrace . . .

Dempsey swung the air cylinders in a sweeping arc. There was a loud clang as they crashed into the side of Ch'ien's head.

Ch'ien acted as if he'd run straight into a tree trunk. He staggered backwards for a short distance then toppled forward and fell on his face.

This time Dempsey wasn't taking any chances. He went over to Ch'ien and swung the air cylinders again. They slammed into Ch'ien's head with a sickening thud. Then Dempsey dropped on his knees beside the Chinaman and tried to get his breath back. His throat hurt terribly and his chest seemed to be on fire. There were coloured lights dancing in front of his eyes and a roaring in his ears. He felt as if he'd fallen off a hundred foot cliff and then been run over a few times by a truck.

Finally, when he was sure he wasn't going to pass out, he reached over and felt Ch'ien's neck. Surprisingly, he found a strong pulse. He'd thought he must have killed him with that final blow.

Moving slowly and painfully he used the straps of the breathing unit to bind Ch'ien's hands and feet together, hog-tying him like a steer.

Then he staggered onto the jetty, peeled off the wetsuit jacket and put on his own clothes. Every movement caused waves of pain to radiate through his body, and bending over was pure agony. He was beginning to suspect he had a couple of broken ribs.

With difficulty he picked up the bag containing the jade and headed up towards the house. Despite all the pain he felt relatively satisfied. He'd recovered the jade and got the guy who'd been working with Naismith. True, there were a few things still to be cleared up, like why Ch'ien had killed Naismith and who Hoffman was . . .

As he entered the house Dempsey paused. He had

intended to take the jade straight up to Makepeace's room, but now it seemed a better idea to hide it somewhere for the time being until all the remaining questions had been resolved. There was still the possibility that a third party might be involved as well as Naismith and Ch'ien. And as absurd as it might seem Dempsey still had his doubts about Lord Winfield.

After all, Naismith had been working for him and he had an extremely strong motive for stealing the jade from himself: to prevent the Chinese getting it.

So Dempsey padded silently into the Great Hall and started to look for a hiding place. He settled for one of the suits of armour. He removed the helmet from one of them and lowered the bag of jade quietly down into the cavity. Replacing the helmet he then made his way up to Makepeace's room.

Her door was slightly ajar. He pushed it open and entered. Makepeace was standing with her back to him at the window.

'Bull's-eye, princess!' he told her. 'I got the jade and I got—' He dried up.

The woman at the window had turned. She was dressed in black and she had blonde hair but she wasn't Makepeace. She was Susan Sims. And she was aiming a .45 automatic right at him.

CHAPTER TWENTY-ONE

'Don't stop on my account,' said Susan Sims. 'Finish what you were saying about the jade.'

'Where is she?' asked Dempsey coldly. He was calculating his chances of drawing his gun and blowing her away before she could fire. But his chances didn't look good. The way she held the .45 suggested she'd had a lot of practice. Besides, his arms were almost numb with fatigue.

'Winfield's daughter?' She gave a cool smile. 'Andy's entertaining her downstairs in the basement. She's fine – so far. Now about the jade. Where is it?'

'I'm not saying a thing until I see Makepeace.'

'Oh dear. And I was hoping we could do it without any fuss. And by the look of you you've had more than enough fuss tonight. Who remodelled your face?'

'You should know,' Dempsey told her. 'You're all working together.'

She gave a puzzled frown. 'I don't follow. Who are you talking about.'

'The Chinese guy, of course.'

She smiled. 'You're way off beam there, Jim. Did you kill him?'

He shrugged. 'Almost.'

'That will amuse the hell out of Andy. Let's go tell him now. But first – put your hands on your head and turn around.'

Dempsey did as she ordered. He tensed, wondering whether he was going to feel the impact of a bullet splintering his spine. But no, he heard her come up behind him, then felt her hand patting the side of his jacket. She quickly found the Magnum and deftly removed it. He heard it land on a chair.

'My, that *is* a big one,' she said with amusement. 'Now get moving but be very careful. Make a twitch I don't like and it's sleepy-bye time.'

Dempsey felt frustratingly helpless as she ushered him downstairs. The hoped-for opportunity to disarm her never presented itself. She was too good, keeping at just the right distance behind him. He tried slowing down a couple of times, hoping to bring her closer but it didn't work.

'Where to now?' he asked her at the bottom of the main staircase.

'Turn left. Head up that passageway towards the kitchens.'

Halfway along it she told him to halt. He was next to a heavy door. She told him to open it. Beyond it a set of stone stairs descended into the darkness.

'There's a light switch on the wall by your right. Turn it on,' said Susan Sims.

The stairs went down a long way. At the bottom Dempsey found himself in a large cellar area. It looked very old, with stone arches supporting the low vaulted ceiling. There were wooden racks of bottles everywhere, most of them covered with dust and cobwebs. If it hadn't been for the few electric light bulbs providing a feeble illumination Dempsey would have sworn he'd gone back in time to the Middle Ages.

'Straight ahead,' came Susan Sims' confident voice from behind him.

He passed between the tall racks of bottles, wondering if he had the time to grab a bottle and use it as a weapon. He dismissed the idea as suicidal.

'Turn right.'

He did so and entered a smaller cellar. What he saw in there made his stomach muscles contract convulsively. He froze.

Makepeace was sitting in a high-backed, wooden chair. She was naked except for her bra and briefs. She was tied to the chair very securely, the thin nylon cord

He returned to the main room and opened the wardrobe. A number of apparently identical Mao jackets and matching trousers hung inside. There was a suitcase on the top shelf and Dempsey was just about to haul it down, when he heard the sound of water dripping on the floor.

He looked down. There was a knapsack on the floor of the wardrobe and water was seeping out of it. He unzipped the top and peered inside.

The knapsack contained a diving mask, two small air bottles, a wetsuit jacket and a pair of flippers. And all of them were dripping wet.

Dempsey pulled the knapsack out and slung it on his back. He started to head for the door then paused and went to the window. As he stared across the shadowy garden he was certain he glimpsed the silhouette of a man creeping through the bushes . . .

Makepeace was running out of places to search. So, reluctantly, she turned her attention to Naismith's body, which was still hanging from the door.

Screwing up her face with distaste she began to feel through his pockets. There was an appalling smell coming from him which didn't make her task any easier. His sphincter muscle had obviously given way at the moment of death.

She quickly built up a small heap of objects on the floor – a wallet, loose change, keys, a driver's licence, notebook, penknife and a biro.

There was a sound behind her. It came from the window. She turned, drawing her .38. The open French windows revealed nothing, just an oblong of impenetrable blackness.

But then she heard the sound again. It wasn't loud. Like a foot scrabbling for a hold just below the balcony. She went into a crouch, holding the .38 in a double-handed grip with both arms fully extended.

biting cruelly into the flesh of her arms, legs and neck. She was very pale but apart from a bruise on her left cheek seemed unharmed. So far.

Next to the chair stood a small metal brazier full of hot coals. A poker protruded from the coals . . .

Behind the chair, his elbows resting on its back, was Andrew Sims. He looked relaxed and at ease. He smiled broadly at Dempsey and said, 'Hey, glad you could make it, Jimmy boy. Now we can start partying for real.'

Dempsey ignored him. 'You okay, princess?'

She gave him a weak smile and said calmly, 'Yes. Apart from the severe dent in my pride. They took me completely by surprise.'

'Hey, it could happen to anyone. Hell, it just happened to me.'

'He's found the jade,' said Susan Sims.

'Yeah?' said her brother, his grin broadening. 'Well, that *is* good news. Where is it now?'

'He won't say.'

'Won't he?' The corners of Sims's mouth turned down in mock sorrow. 'Is that true?' he asked Dempsey.

'I take it you're Hoffman,' said Dempsey.

'He is,' said Makepeace. 'And that's his sister behind you, not his wife.'

With deceptive nonchalance Sims lifted his elbows from the back of the chair and smashed the right one into Makepeace's cheekbone, right where it had been bruised earlier. The blow rocked her head, tightening the cord around her neck. She made a gasping sound as her eyes clouded with pain.

Dempsey flinched as if he'd been hit himself. He wanted to fling himself at Sims and . . .

'Easy, big man,' said Susan, nudging him in the back of his neck with the muzzle of the .45.

'I warned you before to speak only when you're told to,' said Sims to Makepeace. Then to Dempsey he said, 'We been trying to figure out, Sis and I, just how close you and the lady cop here are. Now we reckon you must be in each other's pants on a regular basis but she says your relationship is strictly professional and that you're not even "just good friends" . . .'

'The lady's right,' said Dempsey coldly.

'Yeah? No offence, man, but I find that kinda hard to swallow. A piece like her and a good-looking jock like you. Isn't that right, Sis?'

'Right, Andy.'

'I mean, Jim boy, your lady cop was trying to tell me I could tear her fingernails off in front of you and you wouldn't bat an eyelid. She was exaggerating, right?'

Dempsey said nothing.

'Where's the jade?' asked Sims.

'Don't tell him, Dempsey,' said Makepeace.

Sims stepped out from behind the chair, twisted his body and sent his elbow thudding into Makepeace's upper stomach. Her face went completely white and she tried to double over but, of course, couldn't.

Dempsey clenched his fists.

'Where'd you hide the jade, Jim?' asked Sims again.

'Let her go and I'll tell you.'

'Let her go? No, Jim. Out of the question. Now come on, start talking before I really get rough with her. The jade.'

'Even if I tell you it won't do you any good. The police have this place sealed off. You'll never get away with the stuff.'

'Let me worry about that, Jim boy. Just tell me where it is.'

'No . . .' gasped Makepeace.

Dempsey looked at her, torn with indecision. He had the strong suspicion that once Sims had the jade he'd consider them both to be disposable. So he had to keep stalling for as long as he could.

'I'll tell you where the jade is but first I want some answers.'

'About what?'

'Naismith. Was he working for you or vice versa?'

Sims smiled. He had exceptionally white teeth that contrasted sharply with his deep tan. 'We were kind of partners. Or so he thought. He made us a proposition which we accepted. But naturally we planned to terminate the agreement ahead of schedule.'

'And him too?'

'Yeah. But he was a sharp little operator. He guessed we might try and double-cross him so he took out some insurance. And he made sure we knew he had it.'

'Had what?'

'This.' Sims took some folded papers from his jacket pocket. Dempsey recognized them as the crime sheets from Interpol. 'By the way, thanks for finding them for us.'

'Glad to be of service,' said Dempsey. 'So it was you who nailed him to his door?'

'Yeah. He was getting scared. He was more afraid of me than you. He would have spilled the beans to you to save his neck.'

Dempsey nodded. 'And then you hid your own underwater gear in Ch'ien's room?'

'I thought it would throw you off the track. And it did.'

'Ch'ien has nothing to do with you, or Naismith?'

'Not a thing. He's legit.'

'They had some kind of fight,' Susan Sims told her brother. 'That's why Dempsey looks as if he's been sky-diving without a 'chute.'

'Yeah?' Sims laughed. 'So what happened? You trash the gook?'

'He's in a damaged condition, yeah. But there's one thing I still don't get. Why didn't you recover the jade yourself earlier tonight? Your scuba gear was wet so you'd obviously been in the water.'

'I was, but before I could get started that loony dame comes along and throws herself in the lake . . .'

'Frances Trafford?'

'Yeah. She made a hell of a racket in the water and I

147

was afraid she'd attract unwanted attention, so I got out of there fast.'

'And left her to drown?' said Dempsey coldly.

Sims shrugged. 'When I told Naismith what had happened he started to go to pieces, so I had to get rid of him ahead of schedule. And you know the rest. Now *I* want to know – where is the jade?'

'It's still in the lake,' said Dempsey quickly. 'I hid it under the jetty.'

Sims stared at Dempsey for a time then said, 'How come I got a strong feeling you're lying?'

'I'm not lying. I can take you straight to it.'

'I'll bet you can.'

Sims was wrapping a handkerchief around his hand. he reached for the poker, withdrew it from the coals and, before Dempsey could say anything, suddenly pressed its glowing end against Makepeace's bare upper arm.

There was a sizzling noise and smoke rose into the air. Makepeace screamed. She writhed in agony, struggling vainly against the tight nylon bindings.

Dempsey took a step forward but stopped when he saw Sims move the glowing poker towards Makepeace's left eye.

'You come one more inch closer and I'll shove this through her eye and into her brain,' said Sims casually.

'And enjoy doing it,' Dempsey told him.

Sims grinned. 'Now I'll ask you again – where is the jade?'

'Upstairs. In one of the suits of armour in the main hall.'

Again Sims stared hard at him. But this time he gave a satisfied nod and shoved the poker back into the coals.

'Okay, Jim. Let's go see.' A switchblade appeared in his hand as if by magic and he began to cut through the cords around Makepeace's arms.

When he'd freed her she gave a low moan and slumped forward, clutching at her arm. The smell of her burnt flesh was still heavy in the air. Sims grabbed her

148

hair and yanked her head back up. He put the knife blade to her throat. 'Now listen carefully, both of you. The first hint I get of a wrong move and I do some quick surgery on this nice, white throat here. You got that, Jimmy boy?'

'I got it,' said Dempsey. He was trying to avoid looking directly at Makepeace's face. It was easier keeping his self-control that way. He consoled himself with the thought that one way or another he would kill Sims before sunrise.

'You lead the way, Jim. And try not to trip or anything. I might jump to the wrong conclusion and give your pretty partner here a set of gills before I realize it was unintentional.'

Dempsey's mind raced frantically as the four of them moved in single file through the cellar and then up the stairs. He devised and dismissed a dozen plans during the journey to the Great Hall – all of them were too risky, too chancy. If it had been just his own life at stake he would have been willing to try something rash, but not with Sims holding a knife at Makepeace's throat.

They entered the Great Hall. He indicated the suit of armour that contained the jade.

'You'd better be right, Jim boy,' said Sims.

He was still holding Makepeace by her hair, the switchblade under her chin. Suddenly he pushed her against a wall and stepped away from her. He motioned to Dempsey to join her. Dempsey did so, moving to catch her in his arms as she began to sway on her feet.

'Easy, princess. Take a deep breath . . .'

She clung to him, her body trembling. 'I'll be all right,' she mumbled. He realized that this was the most intimate they'd ever been.

'Okay, break up that touching scene,' ordered Sims. 'Back against the wall, both of you. Sis, one twitch from either of them and you blow them away, you hear?'

Susan Sims, the .45 rock-steady in her hand, nodded and smiled. She looked like a cat about to bite the head off a mouse.

As Sims dismantled the suit of armour Dempsey glanced around at the wide variety of medieval weapons on the walls. If only he could get his hands on just one of them. But how?

Sims gave a small cry of triumph. He held up the plastic bag containing the jade. 'Jackpot,' he told his sister who – professional that she was – hadn't taken her eyes off Dempsey and Makepeace for a fraction of a second.

Grinning widely he came and stood beside his sister and regarded them both cheerfully. 'And now we make tracks – with your help.'

'What do you mean?' asked Dempsey.

'You're going to get us through the road blocks. You're going to flash your cop ID and make up some story about us being in the clear. Or rather, one of you is. We don't need both of you. Question is, which of you do we take?'

'We should take the girl, Andy,' said Susan. 'She'll be easier to handle than the guy and then later we can maybe have some fun with her.'

Sims smiled warmly at his sister. 'As usual, Sis, you cut through the crap and get right down to the nitty-gritty.' He looked at Dempsey and shrugged. 'Sorry, pal. Guess you've drawn the short straw.'

'How we going to kill him?' asked Susan.

'Quietly. Very quietly.'

Sims went and removed a spear from the wall nearby. He hefted it appraisingly in his hands. Dempsey saw it was the twin of the one that had killed Naismith.

'Move away from the girl, Jim,' ordered Sims.

Dempsey obeyed, keeping his eyes on the spear point. He was going to have to rush Sims. He knew it would be a futile gesture – that Sims would skewer him before he even covered a yard – but there was nothing else left to do.

'Bye, Jim,' said Sims. 'This time I'm not going to miss.' He moved in for the kill.

CHAPTER TWENTY-TWO

The metal spearhead would have pierced Dempsey's body at a point just below his heart, but before Sims could drive it home he was sent sprawling sideways by an almost naked, ghost-like figure who had suddenly materialized out of the shadows.

It was Ch'ien.

Dempsey didn't hesitate. As Ch'ien and Sims rolled across the floor, struggling for possession of the spear, he launched himself at Susan, who was already turning to try and get a clear shot at Ch'ien.

He slammed his shoulder into her ribs, knocking her off her feet. She grunted as she fell heavily on her back. Before she had time to raise the .45 Dempsey kicked hard at her hand. The gun went skittering across the floor and vanished into the darkness.

Having disarmed her Dempsey mistakenly assumed the fight was as good as over; he'd forgotten he was dealing with a woman who had the strength and reflexes of a trained athlete. As he bent over her to grab her arms she kicked him in the crutch. For the next few seconds nothing existed for Dempsey except the pain that exploded through him.

As he doubled over, clutching himself, Susan Sims sprang off the floor and delivered a karate chop across the back of his neck. It almost finished him completely. He fell forward onto his hands and knees, helpless, waiting for her next blow.

Someone ran past him. There was the familiar sound of a fist smacking into a face. He turned his head and saw Makepeace follow up her attack with a well-aimed kung-fu kick at Susan Sims' stomach. She doubled over but kept her footing.

Dempsey wanted to cry out a warning to Makepeace; to tell her not to get too close to the woman, but he couldn't get his voice to work. He shook his head to try and clear it of the black, numbing waves that the karate blow on his neck had caused.

Beyond Makepeace and Susan he saw that Ch'ien was still struggling with Sims over the spear, but that Sims was getting the upper-hand. Sims was on top of him, pushing the shaft of the spear down across Ch'ien's throat in an attempt to choke him.

Dempsey knew he had to help one of them, but which one? With an effort he stood up, trying to ignore the pain that racked his body. If only he could find Susan Sims' gun but it was somewhere on the other side of the hall . . .

Makepeace was still on the attack, forcing Susan backwards with a series of kicks, and blows. In her white bra and tiny briefs she looked like some naked Greek Fury out of mythology. He felt a rush of admiration for her; despite everything she'd been through she'd bounced back like a real pro. And along with the admiration were other feelings for her, feelings he immediately pushed into the background.

He turned his attention to Sims and Ch'ien. The Chinaman seemed almost unconscious now as Sims continued to press down on the spear shaft . . .

Dempsey's decision was made for him. He charged Sims in a kind of half-stagger, half-run. Sims heard his approach and started to turn – just in time to get Dempsey's boot in his face.

He let go of the spear, which Ch'ien was still clutching, and went rolling across the floor. Dempsey followed him. It felt as if he'd broken every bone in his right foot but that kick had given him a tremendous feeling of satisfaction.

He got another kick in, against the side of Sims' chest, but this time the toe of his boot seemed to

152

rebound off a wall of solid muscle and he knew he hadn't done any damage.

Sims proved this by then springing to his feet. Blood ran from his split lip, but otherwise he looked disturbingly unharmed.

'Andy!'

It was Susan. Dempsey turned and saw her pull two rapiers from the wall. One she tossed, hilt first, towards her brother.

It never reached him. Makepeace, performing a leap that would have earned her a place in the Royal Ballet Company, snatched it out of the air. She landed nimbly and instantly went into the *en garde* position.

Susan Sims took up a similar position and sneered at her. 'You're out of your league now, bitch. I was the women's foil champion at my college for three years running.'

She lunged with frightening speed and Makepeace just barely managed to parry it.

'Stick her one for me, Sis!' called Sims, then turned and made a grab for something on the wall nearby. When he turned back to face Dempsey he was holding a morning-star; a heavy spiked ball attached to a thick, wooden shaft by a length of chain.

Sims started to whirl it above his head. It made an ominous whistling sound as it cut through the air. Sims grinned at Dempsey, revealing blood-stained teeth.

'I'm gonna splash your brains all over these walls,' he hissed.

Dempsey jumped backwards as Sims tilted the deadly orbit of the metal sphere towards his head. It came so close he felt the breeze of its passage on his face.

Still backing away, Dempsey looked hurriedly around for something to defend himself with before Sims got him trapped in a corner, which was obviously his intention.

153

Suddenly he was falling. His foot had slipped on a round object on the floor. As he keeled backwards, accompanied by a clatter of metal, to his horror he realized he'd stumbled over the pieces from the dismantled suit of armour that had contained the jade.

Sims gave a cry of triumph.

Dempsey's instinct saved him. He rolled to the left just as the spiked ball came whistling down. It smashed into the floorboards with terrifying force, embedding itself in the wood.

The few seconds it took for Sims to yank it free gave Dempsey the chance to get to his feet. As he did so he noticed the shield lying among the bits of armour. He grabbed it and held it up just as Sims freed the morning-star and sent it hurtling towards him again.

The impact of the heavy metal ball on the shield jarred Dempsey's entire body. He staggered backwards, almost losing his balance again. The ball slammed into the shield for the second time, making a loud clang that echoed throughout the Great Hall and causing a jagged tear in the old metal covering of the shield. Again the whistling sound and again *clang!*

Dempsey knew that even with the shield he couldn't withstand this onslaught for much longer. Sims would batter him to the floor and then finish him off. If only he had a weapon . . .

A piercing shriek filled the air. Then Dempsey heard Sims scream '*Sis!*' at the top of his lungs. He lowered the shield and looked.

Makepeace and Susan Sims were frozen together in a grim tableau. Susan was in a lunge position, right leg bent, left leg extended straight behind her, the trunk of her body leaning forward, continuing the line of her left leg, and her sword arm was fully extended as well. But Makepeace had obviously parried the thrust and riposted with unexpected speed because the end of her rapier was sticking through Susan Sims' neck . . .

At that moment Susan stepped back, pulling herself free of Makepeace's sword. Immediately blood began to jet, in rhythmic spurts, out of her throat. She dropped her weapon and clutched vainly at the wound, turning stricken eyes towards her brother.

Then she sank to her knees, making a ghastly bubbling sound, and toppled forward . . .

With a bellow of pain and rage Sims rushed at Makepeace, whirling the morning-star above his head. She retreated, raising the sword to protect herself. But Dempsey could see the rapier would be useless against the ball and chain. Sims had gone beserk; even if she managed to run him through he probably wouldn't notice it.

Dempsey acted fast. He ran to where Ch'ien lay on his back and snatched up the spear. Without waiting to take proper aim Dempsey flung it with all his strength.

It thudded into the small of Sims' back. He screamed and let go of the whirling morning-star, which went flying off on its own, narrowly missing Makepeace before it crashed into a painting on the wall behind her.

Still screaming with pain and anger Sims made a final lunge at Makepeace. She lashed at him with the sword but it didn't stop him. The next thing Dempsey knew Sims had his hands around her throat.

Dempsey charged.

He flung himself on Sims and tore his hands from Makepeace's neck. Then, with a beserk strength of his own, he hurled Sims backwards.

Arms flailing, Sims fell. There was a wet snap and Sims gave one final, agonized scream. The spearhead had been pushed all the way through his body by the force of the fall and now protruded, redly, from his stomach.

He writhed and kicked feebly for a few moments and then was still.

Dempsey, reassured that Sims was finally dead,

155

looked at Makepeace. She was leaning against the wall, all of a sudden looking like a very young and vulnerable child.

Panting hoarsely, he said, 'You OK?'

'No,' she replied in a small voice. She let the rapier fall from her hand. It clattered loudly on the floor.

He went to her. 'That was real fancy swordplay you dished out back there.'

'I was a foils champion at my college too,' she told him. 'But she was just careless – too over-confident. She practically ran on my sword all by herself.' She put her arms around him. 'Hold me. I don't feel very well.'

'I'm not feeling too hot myself, princess,' he said as he embraced her. 'But look on the bright side; we're alive and they ain't.'

She looked up at him. 'You saved my life.'

'And you saved mine earlier, so we're even.'

Unexpectedly, Makepeace kissed him. Hard, on the mouth. Dempsey was so surprised that for a few seconds he just stood there, as responsive as a store window dummy. Then he began to reciprocate . . .

'I say, what on earth is going on down here?' the voice boomed loudly in the Great Hall.

Makepeace and Dempsey broke hurriedly apart and turned. Standing on the main staircase and peering at them through the gloom was Lord Winfield. He was clutching a golf putter in one hand and a walking stick in the other.

'Good Lord, *Harry!*' he cried when he recognized his daughter. Then, after noticing she was dressed only in her underwear, he said, 'Harry, what fun and games you get up to around here at night are strictly your business, but do you have to make such a damned awful racket about it?'

Makepeace started to laugh. And after a pause Dempsey joined in.

Lord Winfield stared at them uncomprehendingly.

156

'We do look as if we've been through the wars. All of us,' observed Lord Winfield.

It was late afternoon and the four of them, Lord Winfield, Ch'ien, Makepeace and Dempsey, were sitting in the study. It was the first quiet moment any of them had had all day. Since early morning Winfield Hall had been filled with police officers, but now the last of the police vehicles had departed and a semblance of calm had returned to the estate.

Dempsey glanced at the others and nodded his agreement with Lord Winfield. All of them were displaying facial injuries, the most spectacular of which were Ch'ien's. One side of his face was grossly swollen and there was an egg-sized lump on the top of his shaven head. Makepeace looked the least damaged. Skilful application of make-up concealed most of the bruising on her cheek, and the bandages on her arm were hidden under the sleeve of her blouse. She was looking her usual cool and poised self.

'I feel like the guy in that movie, *Ben Hur*,' said Dempsey. 'The one who lost the chariot race and got trampled on by every damn horse in the arena.' He gingerly touched his bruised chin and looked accusingly at Ch'ien. 'I got you to thank for a lot of these lumps, Mr Ch'ien.'

Ch'ien smiled painfully, touching the swelling on his face. 'And I have you to thank for this, Mr Dempsey. You are truly a formidable opponent. Very few people have ever bested me in physical combat. In fact you almost succeeded in killing me.'

'Thank God I didn't, or Makepeace and I probably

wouldn't be here now. And thank God you managed to get free of those straps I hog-tied you with.'

Ch'ien smiled again. 'Fortunately your ability with knots does not equal your prowess as a fighter. But it is a pity we fought at all. For that I must humbly take the blame. A distressing case of mistaken identity and unforgivably careless of me.'

'Hey, don't blame yourself,' said Dempsey. 'I'd have done the same. Hell, Sims practically arranged it to happen that way.'

Lord Winfield gave a deep sigh. 'If we're apportioning the blame for all this mess, then I must take my fair share for ever placing my trust in Naismith. He obviously had the wool pulled over my eyes completely. I still find it hard to believe he planned the whole thing.'

'He sure did, Lord Winfield,' said Dempsey. 'When he learned that the jade was most likely going to be returned to China he took steps to have it stolen. He had a lot of underworld connections and through them he got in contact with the Sims . . .'

'And bit off more than he could chew,' said Makepeace.

'And you say he was actually blackmailing poor Frances as well?' asked Lord Winfield.

Dempsey nodded. 'Naismith had found out her husband had committed suicide after learning of her affairs. He was threatening to tell her husband's family unless she played ball.'

'Poor Frances,' said Lord Winfield. 'I'll miss her. She was a dear friend.'

'Is there any way you can use your influence to keep that part of the story out of the newspapers, Daddy?' asked Makepeace.

'I'll do my best, dear. I'll certainly do my best. In a way I suppose I'm partly responsible for her suicide. Because of my bad judgement in hiring Naismith I made it possible for him to get his evil hooks into her.'

Dempsey took a long swallow of his drink and said, 'I feel bad about her too, Lord Winfield. If I hadn't left her alone that night she might still be alive.'

There was silence in the study. Somewhere in the distance they heard a door slam.

Dempsey said, 'I guess you'll have two of them around from now on.'

Makepeace frowned. 'Two what?'

'Ghosts,' said Dempsey. 'Two Black Widows.'

'How's your arm?' Dempsey asked Makepeace as they drove up the hillside road that led away from Winfield Hall.

'A bit sore,' she replied vaguely.

He glanced at her. She was staring out the window with a frown on her face. 'Something bothering you?' he asked.

There was a long pause before she answered. 'Dempsey, about what happened . . .' She didn't go on.

'Yeah?'

'About what happened when we . . . you know . . .'

'No,' he said, though he did know.

'I'm talking about after the fight. When I . . . I kissed you . . .'

He glanced at her again. She was looking directly ahead, determined not to meet his eyes. 'Yeah. What about it?'

'I don't want you to get the wrong idea. It happened because I was . . . upset. Shaken. Very badly shaken . . .'

'So was I.'

'You understand then? You're not going to jump to any wrong conclusions?'

'About what?'

'About why I kissed you.'

He shrugged. 'I don't even know what you're talking about, princess.'

She did look at him then, her eyes narrowing with suspicion. He gave her an innocent smile. She looked away.

After several minutes of silence between them Dempsey said, 'There is one thing, princess.'

'Yes?' she asked, a hint of nervousness in her voice.

'You think your father will object to having an American for a son-in-law?'

For a few moments Makepeace was too stunned to respond. Then she exploded with a series of expletives, some of which were new even to Dempsey.

He started to laugh. He was still laughing when they reached London.